SHIFTING LOOT

SHIFTING LOOT

DANIELLE FORREST

The Eternal Scribe Publishing
Indianapolis, IN

PRONUNCIATIONS

- Kou - Coo
- Surg - Surge
- Diehli - Day-lee
- Baeki - Bay-key
- Lycaon - Lycan
- Hacht - Hacked
- Ateles - Ah-tell-ease

Chad Sexington dashed backward, dodging a blow from his right. With a cockiness he couldn't contain, he easily blocked the next attack, winking at the girl behind him. Then he kicked his foe, knocking them back as he pulled out his blaster and fired. The alien slammed into the wall, its green blood smearing against the surface.

He spun around, gun still raised. The girl squealed, her breasts jumping enticingly as he pulled the trigger. She screamed, then froze as the last alien dropped dead. She looked behind her, then back at Chad. "You saved me," she said breathlessly.

He smirked, stepping up to invade her personal space. "That I did. How would you like to reward me?"

Eyebrows raising, she smiled back, running a single finger down the center of his chest, the silky material of his shirt only adding to the sensual caress. "Oh, I could think of some ways."

He wrapped his arms around her. "Why don't you show me?"

She leaned up and snaked her arms around his neck. "Maybe I will." She pressed her lips to his, sneaking her tongue inside.

"Oh, gross, Cass," Jessie said, jarring Cassandra out of the moment.

Cass dropped her feet from their perch on the console and turned around to face her younger sister. "What?"

"Could you *not* have Angus read your smut novels aloud in the cockpit? You have a bedroom, for crying out loud!" Still just a teenager, Jessie's thin arms flew up in the air.

"I could…"

"Then why don't you?" Jessie's shoulders hunched forward, the cut of her bright purple shirt accentuating her budding breasts, much to Cass's chagrin. God, when did her little sister grow up?

She still remembered when their parents abandoned them, leaving the responsibility of caring for her sister on her teenaged shoulders. It had been too much, but it hadn't stopped her. She would never forget the look on Jessie's face when their parents didn't return. "Where's mama?" two-year-old Jessie had said, who was still living as a boy back then. The hurt, lost look in Jessie's eyes had gutted her, leaving her determined to do whatever it took to keep them together.

It hadn't been easy. Barely an adult herself, she hadn't known what the fuck she was doing, let alone how to care for a little kid. Things had been hard, nightmarish really, until they'd found the shifter community. That caravan had saved them. No more crappy apartments with pest infestations. No more working two jobs while Jessie stayed home by herself. No more worrying about what might happen while she wasn't there to watch her.

"What did you say?" she asked, having lost track of the conversation.

Jessie glared, propping her fists on her hips. "I said, 'Why don't you?' "

Right. She shrugged, then smirked. "Probably because I'd be too tempted to masturbate, then I'd get *nothing* done."

Jessie's face screwed up. "Oh gross!"

Gross, indeed. She rolled her eyes, enjoying the exaggerated facial expressions and mannerisms her sister gave her.

God, I love her.

Jessie stepped forward, her long brown hair bouncing in its ponytail. "So, were you working before you got distracted?"

Cass smirked at her before facing the console once more. "I had Angus running a search on likely places to scope out targets."

Jessie nodded, leaning over her chair. "Any hits?"

Cass ran her hand over the display where the search had been running. "Yup, got one. A planet, relatively low traffic on the port, minimal security, and we haven't hit it before. Should be an easy in and out. Low risk, too."

"Good. How long?"

"Two days travel time in sub-space."

"Kay. Heading for the kitchen. I'm *starving*," Jessie said before skipping out of the room.

Cass looked behind her, smiling at her sister.

I love you.

"We will be landing in five minutes," Angus's thick Scottish brogue called over the intercom.

Cass left her bedroom, heading toward the cockpit. She smiled at the hallway, where she'd let Jessie paint the walls years ago. Formerly plain metal walls, it was now navy blue with pinpoint stars and planets drawn out in intricate detail. Her sister was such an artist.

The cockpit, on the other hand, was fairly boring, though they'd both given it their individual flairs. The consoles limited their ability to personalize, but their chairs had been decorated. Jessie's was purple with stars on it. Cass's was decorated with nebulas, something she'd always found beautiful.

She dropped into her seat and strapped in, calling out behind her. "Jess! Get your ass in here and buckle up. I don't want you flying around the ship like a pinball!"

"Bitch!" Jessie yelled back.

Cass rolled her eyes, but couldn't say anything. It was her own damn fault. She'd never bothered to cut back her cursing around Jess, and the girl had lapped up every obscene word.

Granted, as a pirate, nobody expected them to speak all prim and proper. But had she done her sister a disservice? Looking back over her shoulder at the intricately painted hallway, she wondered if Jess could have done something more socially acceptable with her life.

When at least a minute passed without Jess showing, Cass yelled down the hallways again. "Jess! Get your ass in here!"

"Come *on!*" Jess said, her voice growing closer. "I'm coming already. God, you're so impatient."

"Comes with the territory, babe." After all, pirates didn't have any virtues to speak of.

Finally, Jess showed up, moving slowly down the hallway.

"If you move any slower, we'll be landed by the time you reach the cockpit."

"Yeah, right." Jess waved her hand in front of her and rolled her eyes.

"Just hurry up and get buckled in."

"On it," Jess said as she rounded her chair and dropped in place. "So, same old, same old?"

"Yup. I investigate possible ships, and you monitor security channels with Angus."

"Come on, Cass! What the fuck! You *know* Angus could do that all by himself. He's a fucking AI, for crying out loud!"

"Jess…"

"No," she shook her head. "You should take me with you. I could help. I could watch your back."

Cass opened her mouth to refuse, but stopped, considering it for the first time. Jess wasn't a baby anymore. Though not quite an adult either, she could help. "Fine, you can watch my back." She looked down at Jess's outfit, a belly shirt with a plunging neckline and booty shorts. "But you're changing your clothes first."

"What the fuck, Cass!"

She held up her hand. "Non-negotiable. Part of the job is portraying the right image. We want to blend." She waved her hand up and down Jess's body. "That doesn't blend."

Jess looked down and chuckled. "No, I suppose it doesn't."

"Descending to the planet's surface," Angus said, his brogue thick and dreamy. Her friend, Ellie, might complain constantly about Angus's heavy accent, but she loved it. It was just a pity

Ellie could hardly understand him, and he was installed on her ship, too.

Well, too bad. Years ago, Victoria, who'd designed their three ships, had asked Cass to program the AI, knowing it would be needed for sub-space travel. Cass had happily agreed, loving being able to use her computer skills for something other than hacking for a change, a skillset that had kept them afloat in those early years when minimum wage jobs just didn't cut it.

Suddenly, the force of entering atmosphere shoved her back in her seat. She gripped the armrests, waiting for the force to let off.

The viewscreen flared red, and the planet's surface grew before them.

"Damn, that planet sucks," Jess said beside her.

She couldn't disagree. The surface reminded her a bit of Tatooine, though it had the dark mass of a city center off to the right. Up ahead, a large ocean loomed, but they passed that by far too quickly. She checked the display. Two more laps of the planet before they'd slowed down sufficiently to land.

The ocean disappeared, and the sands returned. The enormous desert covered almost eighty percent of the planet. She couldn't imagine living here, and it seemed obvious why there was so little traffic. On the second lap, she spotted an enormous waste field not far from the ocean's shore. Brine waste from converting the ocean's salt water into drinking water. Highly toxic. Very dangerous.

These people were nuts.

Finally, they slowed, and the port came into view. It doubled as a sea and space port. In the distance, large ships loaded down with cargo containers waited just offshore, the seemingly endless sea all you could see behind them. Below, a handful of spaceships sat parked, and people scurried about, resembling ants from this height.

"This is Flight Control. Please state your name and purpose."

"This is Captain Cassandra Allen of the *Trojan*." She held in a chuckle. She always got a kick out of the name. First, because of the classical reference no alien would ever pick up on. Second, because of the brand of condoms. Yeah, no one would ever say she didn't have a dirty mind. "Just a short stop-off to stretch our legs and restock."

"Cleared to land."

"Thank you, Flight Control."

"Sending your landing coordinates now."

"Thanks again." She sat back, shaking her head at how easy this was. How come no one was ever suspicious of them? Were they really that good, or was everyone really that damn gullible?

Wind howled around the ship as the thrusters lowered them to the ground. Because Angus was driving and not Cass, they dropped to the ground with nary a bump. She smirked self-deprecatingly. Cass could fly, but she had a bit of a lead foot, so to speak. She never seemed to manage anything short of full speed ahead. Jess had banned her from landing the ship *years* ago.

"We've landed. You're free to move about the ship again," Angus said.

"Thank you, Angus," they said in unison, causing Jess to giggle.

Cass smiled over at her sister before popping her harness and pushing herself out of her seat. "Time to get to work. Jess, change."

"Are you changing?" she asked, still buckled in.

Cass looked down at herself. She wore a long sleeved black shirt and cargo pants. "What's wrong with this?"

"Well, you look like a commando."

Cass laughed. "With this hair?" She flicked her purple pixie cut. The bright color teased the edges of her vision.

Jess rolled her eyes. "Maybe wear a hat."

Cass scuffed Jess's head, messing up the neat ponytail. "Brat. Fine, I'll put on a hat." She jogged down the hall, her combat boots clapping against the metal plates. She stopped at her door, pushing it open. Hers was the largest bedroom on the ship, not that you could tell from the mess. Hopping over discarded clothes that took up every inch of the floor, she stumbled over a shoe hidden in the pile and fell against the unmade bed.

"Fuck." Leaning against the bed, she looked around. A table and two chairs sat to the right of the door. Thank God she didn't have any dirty dishes on it when they landed. An image popped into her head of moldy food flung all over the clothes on the floor. She didn't relish cleaning *that* up again.

On the far side of the room, a desk waited. The papers she'd left there were strewn across the floor along with her tablet, which looked fine on its pile of cushioning cloth.

"There," she said, rolling across the bed to the nightstand. She grabbed the drawer where the edge of her hat peeked out. The drawer didn't budge. Vicky had designed it to lock in place so it didn't pop open during launch or landing, but the hat had jammed it. "Come on," she grumbled, putting her back into it.

When the drawer gave up the ghost, she fell on the floor, the impact jarring her even *with* the cushioning. "I seriously need to clean up this mess." She pulled the hat out, a black baseball cap with a single white "A" on it, and slammed the drawer closed, making sure it stayed that way.

Swinging her arms back and forth, she crossed the floor, cognizant that *anything* could live beneath the visible surface. "I *really* need to clean up this shit."

"Hat, Cass. Goes *on* your head," Jess said as she left her room across from Cass's.

"Smartass," Cass said while she put the hat on, drawing it tight to her skull. It felt uncomfortable, constricting. She liked her pixie cut. It felt free. She valued her freedom. "Better?"

Jess shrugged. "I guess."

"Brat," Cass said, wrapping an arm around her sister's shoulder. She didn't really mean it this time.

They walked down the hallway. Thanks to Angus, the exterior door opened as they approached. The heat blasted them from several feet away, and Cass's eyes immediately felt dry.

"So, what do we do?" Jess said, bumping Cass's arm.

"First, we keep our voices down. We don't want anyone overhearing something they shouldn't."

Jess rolled her eyes and gestured at the almost empty port. "Do you *see* anyone who could hear us?"

Cass pointed at Jess's nose. "Don't ever assume that no one can hear or see you just because you don't know they're there. The universe is complex and vast, far more than we could ever imagine. Expect the unexpected."

Jess nodded, solemn for once. The usual bounce in her step disappeared as she scanned the surrounding area. They stepped off the ramp, neither of them speaking.

Even through the thick soles of her boots, she felt the heat of the desert sands. In places, the sand crackled where ship engines had melted the granules, turning them to glass. She kept her head on a swivel as they walked through the port, passing ship after ship. Each one had a different design, coming from different cultures, different species.

Some were sleek, all smooth angles that looked graceful in the blistering sun, light shining brightly off their surfaces. Others were blunt, with harsh angles that made them almost seem angry, like those angles were weapons to fight their enemies with. Even the colors varied. Many ranged from white to black or various metallic tints, but others had been painted, every color of the rainbow represented.

But she didn't focus too much on the design or aesthetics. She focused on more important aspects. She discarded one ship because its paint was peeling away. Another, she discounted because the engines looked like they were on their last leg. She was looking for something in particular. They needed to find a ship in a good state of repair, and not just because it was more likely to have something worth stealing. If the ship wasn't in good condition, she could end up killing people, and she didn't want that on her conscience.

Then she saw it. The ship looked a little worn around the edges, but in good shape. She lingered nearby, chatting idly with her sister as she watched. The cargo bay door opened, belching out several members of the crew just a few feet away. Her heart rate kicked up, but she reminded herself she had nothing to fear. She was doing nothing suspicious. They wouldn't notice her. They never did.

The crew wore a single uniform, but not military. Most looked like academics followed by one man she would swear was the captain and another she openly gawked at, who had the distinctive presence of someone with military training.

And damn, was he dreamy. He was obviously the same species as Ellie's beau, Zee. He wore dark tinted goggles to protect his eyes from the harsh sunlight. Unlike Zee, his charcoal gray hair was short and only covered half his scalp. Exposed metal covered the entire left side of his head.

Cass waited in expectant silence, more than happy to lap up the eye candy while she waited. *Hot damn, look at those muscles.* He was big, looked even bigger than Zee, and Zee was fucking man candy. This guy looked like he would tower over a girl and make her feel tiny, and since Cass was almost six feet tall herself, that wasn't easy to do.

Finally, the group wandered off, leaving Cass and Jess to their business. She sidled up to a panel by the cargo bay door and looked at Jess knowingly. Jess nodded and saluted with a smirk, turning her back on her sister.

Cass returned to the panel, ready to work her magic. She dug in her cargo pants pockets, pulling out a device and a bundle of wires. She fiddled with the bundle until she found a connector that matched the small port on the panel. Popping the cable in her mouth, she shoved the rest back and hooked up her "cracker," a little something she'd designed to install a backdoor in practically any system. Since perfecting it a few years ago, she'd yet to have it fail her.

The light on the cracker turned green, and she grinned, disconnecting it and shoving it in her pocket once more. She turned to her sister. "We're in business. Let's go."

Kou squinted his eyes, the nagging headache forming even with the so-called UV blocking sunglasses on. The world was washed out, like an overexposed image. He ran his hand over his scalp, self-conscious of the bald spot left over from a mission that nearly took his life. He was glad to be alive, but at what cost? Kou constantly reminded himself that it was an honor to be a cyborg, that they were respected on his home world, Ateles, but he had a hard time believing it.

Instead, every time he touched the metal, every time he felt the uneven fall of hair, every time he saw himself in the mirror, he felt like a failure. The mission had failed. He'd lost the left side of his face, his left arm, and most of the skin and muscle on the left side of his body, but his unit had lost their lives. He'd been the only one to survive.

I failed them.

Maybe that was why he didn't live or work on Ateles anymore. He couldn't bear the respect people gave him for what he saw as his greatest failure. At least his crew didn't mention it, one way or the other. They didn't give him undue respect for it, but they didn't turn in disgust, either. It was the best he could hope for, really.

"Let's move," the captain said, leading their small team to collect the package they'd come for.

Kou touched the guns at his sides as he scanned their surroundings. Spaceships overwhelmed the open space. In the distance, an engine roared, while somewhere closer, unseen voices discussed repairs. Other than a woman and child loitering nearby, there was no one within sight. No threats. Of course, he didn't expect any. Not yet, at least. It wasn't until *after* they retrieved the package that he expected trouble.

He frowned, not happy with the security on this mission. He would have preferred an entire team, but it was just him. It wasn't enough, not if someone really tried something. He could only do so much, and he'd already proven himself a failure.

He didn't want to fail again.

Cass stepped into the *Trojan*, her sister on her heels.

"Did we do good? Did you see me?" Jess bounced around, a big smile on her face.

Cass shook her head, trying not to laugh at her sister's antics. Sometimes, it was hard to remember she was almost an adult. "You did okay. Now the fun begins."

Jess rolled her eyes as they headed toward the cockpit. Cass's bedroom had a better setup, but remembering the near face plant she'd done earlier, she didn't want to risk it until she cleaned up a little.

Like that's gonna happen.

"For you, maybe," Jess said as she trudged along at Cass's heels, her feet stomping against the metal flooring. She swore her little sister had perfected her step to maximize the sound it made as she walked.

Cass shrugged. "I like computers, so sue me."

"Wake me when it's over."

"Sure kiddo. You don't have to watch me, you know." She smirked over her shoulder.

Jess had stopped in the middle of the hallway. "Okay, bye." She dashed in the opposite direction, disappearing into their tiny galley kitchen.

She's gonna eat us out of house and home.

Cass continued on to the cockpit and sat in her nebula seat, cracking her knuckles with a grin on her face. "Okay, time to play."

She brought up the console display, setting up the viewscreen for additional real estate, then pulled up her cracking program. It probably wasn't anything special, just a little something she'd come up with to make her jobs easier. Still, she held a certain fondness for it, like it was a grand accomplishment.

With a swipe of her hand, she moved the dashboard she would use during the heist to the main viewscreen and returned to the tiny display before her. Reaching in her pocket, she powered on her cracker. It automatically recognized the *Trojan*'s systems and connected, giving her the backdoor sequence into her target's ship.

Since each ship, each system, was different, she couldn't create a single simple program for all. The cracker had been a labor of love, a complex algorithm spanning dozens of programming languages, all of which she had to learn from scratch. But here, she linked her backdoor manually to her dashboard, so when the time came, she just needed to press a button.

So much easier than trying to code on the fly.

CHAPTER TWO

Cass sat back and watched as Angus tracked their target. They were in sub-space, which she'd always found a bit trippy. On the viewscreen, it looked like half the current solar system had exploded, resulting in a kaleidoscope of colors and shapes. It was dangerous and a bitch to navigate, which was why there were no manual controls for sub-space on this ship except during emergencies.

She was sort of glad. With her lead foot, she could only imagine the hijinks she could get herself into.

Jess hovered over her shoulder, anxious to get started, which wasn't going to happen until they were well and ready. She was waiting until she didn't have to worry about some good samaritan stumbling on their target ship and trying to help.

That meant distance.

Cass was tempted to have Angus read some more of her book, but Jess would be pissed. A smirk crossed her face, and she began to chuckle.

"What's so funny?" Jess said as she pushed away and found her seat, lounging across the armrest.

"I was just thinking I could read a book to pass the time." Her smirk grew.

Jess jerked in her seat, sputtering in outrage. "Do it, and I'll strangle you in your sleep." Her voice squeaked as she fumbled into a more upright seated position. Her index finger waved in Cass's face. "I'm warning you."

The warning fell flat, though, considering how long Jess's gangly limbs had flailed in the air. Cass burst out laughing, holding her stomach as she lost it, her face and sides starting to hurt. "Stop. Stop," she wheezed, but the merriment didn't end.

Eventually, she did stop, but Jess was glaring at her, looking every inch the teenager she was.

"Okay, okay, I'm sorry. I won't laugh again."

"It's not funny," Jess said, looking away. "How much longer?" she asked, changing the subject.

Cass looked down at the console, then out at the swirling eddies of space. They'd been flying for maybe half an hour now, nowhere near long enough, really. But she couldn't blame her sister for being impatient. It was hard waiting, and Cass had never been the patient sort.

"We'll be there before you know it."

***

Kou sat in his quarters, a tiny room that included a foldaway bed too small for his large frame, a built-in desk and monitors, and storage cubbies against the back wall.

It was small and utilitarian, and it left him with a desperate urge to *move*. He'd been a soldier for years before the military retired him. Back then, he'd been grateful, but in times like these, he missed being so active.

Kou sat at his desk, running scans of the surrounding space, making sure they weren't followed. He knew full well there were those who would love to get their hands on the package they'd just collected.

Kou leaned back, rubbing the fuzzy side of his face. *The only side of his face.* He didn't think of the metal as part of him, even if he could sense everything almost the same as his biological side. He dropped his hand away and sighed, realizing he was depressing himself again.

Best not to think about it.

That had been his motto for some time now. It never seemed to work. No matter what he did, his mind always seemed to return to that fateful mission and the fact that he'd returned from it less than a man.

Kou crouched behind cover, rifle in hand, waiting out the enemy fire. Beside him, his superior officer held up a hand, counting down until they would strike. He'd already given them directions. Now, they waited.

Surprisingly, his heart didn't even ramp up at that hacht of a mission. They were cornered, outmanned, outgunned, and he was pretty sure they were all going to die, but try telling their unit leader that. He only looked at them with a cheeky grin before giving the signal to strike.

Kou burst from cover, raising his weapon to eye-level. Pop, pop, pop. *The weapon jerked in his hands as he laid down cover fire for the others. He fired ceaselessly, trying to keep the enemy from firing back. Time dragged on, slowing to a crawl as he fought on.*

For a time, they seemed almost to be winning. As he watched, the enemy fell by their weapons, by their hands, with far fewer of his own falling in kind. They crept across the desolate landscape, passing gray, cracked rocks and kicking up dust on the barren ground. They crawled forward like an unstoppable tide. Hope started to bloom in his chest.

We've got this.

Then the unthinkable happened. A voice to his left shouted, "Incoming!" He looked up. His mind registered the arcing object above their heads, that it had started coming down to his left, but his brain was slow to process the information, to warn him of its significance.

Grenade.

He recognized the familiar design a moment too late. If he'd reacted faster, he could have tried to dive for cover. If he'd reacted faster, he could have dragged someone with him. There'd been a large rock to his right. He could have made it.

He didn't.

The explosive hit the ground, detonating and taking most of his body with it.

Kou shivered and shook his head. He rubbed his temples, trying to drive the images out. "No. Don't." Why did he keep doing this to himself? Why couldn't he let it go, move on? He couldn't have saved anyone, he reminded himself. Hell, it was a miracle *he'd* survived that blast.

Taking a deep breath, he focused back on the displays. "Keep your mind on the job," he reminded himself out loud. "The job."

In the upper corner, a warning icon blinked, and he clicked it. It pulled up a message. "Unknown object detected."

He tapped it, and a details page came up, showing everything the scan had found. There was nothing on the standard scans, but the computer systems were receiving a glitch, a flickering signal it couldn't identify.

Kou frowned. It might be nothing, might just be signal noise, but better safe than sorry. He set up an alert on his watch in case the scans could track a more definitive signal.

With a yawn, he stood, stretching his long body. He'd always been tall and big, bigger than most Ateles, a fact he'd reveled in at one time, but not anymore. He felt compelled to start a patrol, needing to check that everything was in order.

The crew often laughed at him for his vigilance, but he didn't think it was unwarranted. They would laugh, tell him, "We're in space. Nobody can get on board without us knowing," but Kou didn't trust in that. People *could* board a ship undetected, which was why he was suspicious of the scan glitch.

Better safe than sorry.

Cass cracked her knuckles, leaning back in her seat. Jess bounced beside her, ready for the party to start. On the display before her, a big green button said, "Go."

"It's time." They'd left the main trading routes some time ago, and she didn't think anyone would stumble on them all the way out here. She pressed the button. "Angus, you know the drill."

"Aye, lass. Give it ten minutes for the crew to pass out, then initiate the docking procedure."

"Right you are, you sexy man beast." She propped her heels on the console and leaned back, folding her arms behind her head. "Now, what could we *ever* do to pass the time?"

"No smut novels," Jess said, glaring.

Cass rolled her eyes. "God, you're no fun. How did I ever raise such a prude?"

"God only knows."

Cass sighed. "Angus, maybe play some music?"

"Aye, lass." A moment later, her favorite rock music came through the speakers.

"Thanks, Angus." Though, she would have preferred the smut. She'd always liked the cocky, sexy Chad Sexington. Sure, the series was a bit of a parody. His name said it all, but it was fun, and it helped pass the time between ports.

Certainly, that was her least favorite part of being a space pirate—long dry spells while she was out in space with nothing but her sister for company. And while Angus had a sinfully sexy voice, he didn't have the body to go with it, which was no fun at all. God, what she wouldn't give for a few good rounds of hide the salami right about now.

It had been too long since the last time they'd stopped at a port for long enough to hit it off with someone. Cass wasn't terribly picky. She liked 'em big and muscular, but she wasn't looking for a relationship, so didn't care about things like personality. And species didn't really matter either. Sometimes, weird just made it all the more interesting. Why have a boring old human when you can have someone with tentacles? Or two dicks?

And then some of the types of dicks out there… It just left a girl wanting to comparison shop. Often enough, when she found herself in a bar, and she spotted a species she'd never done it with before, she immediately started wondering what he had in his pants and then promptly endeavored to find out.

Sometimes, she was disappointed, but that came with the territory. Some guys were duds, but that was okay. There were always more fish in the sea. And the universe was a damn big sea.

She yawned as she waited to begin. Unfortunately, this part always sucked. They needed to wait for the atmospherics on the target ship to drop low enough for the crew to lose consciousness. Then, they could dock, use her handy program to bypass the security protocols on the target's airlock, and board.

All in all, it was a fairly foolproof setup, allowing them to hijack the ship and steal the goods without a single person getting hurt. Hell, technically, they didn't even need to bring weapons with them, though she always insisted. "Come on, Jess," she said, dropping her feet to the floor with a clap of sound. "Let's get geared up."

"Aye, aye, captain," she said with a sarcastic grin.

They left the cockpit and walked the central hallway to the "cargo bay," which had become a workspace of sorts. She'd subdivided the space, creating smuggling holds on the right and gear walls on the left. Cass moved to the left, stopping in front of a spot midway down the wall. She grabbed her thigh holsters, strapping them in place, then reached for her armored jacket. She slipped it on, adjusting it until it fit snugly without impairing range of motion. Then, she grabbed her bracer and HUD. The bracer, she put on her left wrist, holding down on the screen to power it up. It was her connection to the *Trojan* and Angus. The HUD wrapped around her head with a holographic display over her right eye. Lastly, she grabbed the portable rebreather that would keep them conscious on the target ship.

She turned to her sister. Jess didn't have guns or holsters, only the same armored jacket. Cass'd never taken Jess onto a target ship before, so she'd never given her more than that. The jacket was just a worst-case scenario sort of thing. She shuddered at the idea of a target boarding their ship with her sister unprotected within.

"Ready?" Cass asked as she fiddled with Jess's jacket.

"As ever." Jess shrugged.

"Angus? Status?"

"Will initiate docking in two minutes."

"Thank you, Angus." She turned to a door by the back wall. The airlock was in the cargo bay, a setup she'd always thought was strange. Why the cargo bay? But then, remembering how the ship functioned, she supposed it made sense. In order to simulate gravity, the ship rotated constantly on a central axis. It would be damned difficult to dock with a moving target like that.

They stood outside the metal door. A control panel sat to the right, its display showing various options. She rolled her eyes like her sister often did. Leave it to Vicky to make things overly complicated.

"Prepare for cessation of artificial gravity," Angus said over the intercom.

They both reached out for the wall, grabbing the vertical grab bars that framed the door. A few moments later, her body's hold on the floor disappeared, and she started to float.

Clunk.

"Airlock secured. Please wait. Overriding security protocols."

She bit down harder on the rebreather, but continued breathing through her nose.

"Protocols overwritten. Opening airlock doors. Reestablishing artificial gravity." With a gentle pull, her feet dropped to the metal plates once more.

The door slid up, disappearing into its frame. Cass pushed through.

Hope they have something good.

<hr>

Kou frowned. The air felt thinner, his right lung burning a little. Was life support acting up? The captain kept the ship in pretty good repair, so he found it doubtful, but still. He shouldn't be breathing so hard from just walking down the metal corridors.

Then the artificial gravity gave out, and he shot out a hand, grabbing a groove in the wall. "Hacht." He floated in the air for a short spell before gravity reasserted itself. What was that?

He didn't like it. Acid churned in his gut as he checked his watch, which said, "Cannot Connect."

Not good…

"Captain?" he yelled, moving faster down the hall toward the bridge. He passed empty rooms, ignoring them in favor of getting to the control center of the ship as fast as possible, where he knew answers waited. But he didn't get that far. He turned the corner and skidded to a halt, his shoes squeaking against the floor tiles.

Kou kneeled down next to the body on the ground, his old insecurities rising once more. Had he failed? Was she dead? He didn't know the researcher very well. He couldn't even say what species she was. Her teal skin varied in places from blue to green and always looked slick, like she'd just come out of the water. Her large mouth gaped open, panting, which alarmed him. Didn't someone say her species could hold their breath for long periods of time? Why was she short of breath?

She was paler than usual, too, probably from lack of oxygen, and suddenly the burning in his right lung made perfect sense.

Life support *was* acting up, but his cybernetic parts could compensate for the lack.

Hacht.

He stood and broke into a run, heading for the bridge. He had to solve this *now*, or the whole crew would die.

"So, what now?" Jess asked, her voice sounding thin.

Cass glared at her little sister. "Keep your rebreather in. What's wrong with you?" Even that short stint with the rebreather in her hand had left her breathless. Damn.

She motioned toward the left, her HUD giving her a red overlay of the ship's layout. They couldn't know where the best goods would be, but certain places tended to be safe bets.

Cass started for the cargo bay first. People usually kept sellable goods there. She ignored the aesthetics of the ship as she searched for trouble. All the crew should be out cold, but some species had different life support needs, and people weren't the only things that could turn a job FUBAR.

So far, she hadn't heard any movement or alarming sounds. Nor were there any funky smells that might mean something was about to blow or asphyxiate them.

As she approached a door near the end of the hall, her HUD indicated it led to the cargo bay. It was plain and black, a smooth brushed metal that did little to break up the monotony. She lifted her left wrist, looking down at her bracer. It had situational control, meaning its primary options reflected her position. She tapped, "Open door." The door clanged, and she bumped it with her shoulder. She didn't go any farther, a frown marring her face.

Nothing.

She'd never seen a cargo bay so empty. No, that wasn't true. When Vicky first gave her the *Trojan*, it was this empty. The expanse had seemed daunting, too big. Probably why she ended up subdividing. She didn't have a lot of use for huge open space.

This reminded her of that moment years ago, staring at the abyss before her. It didn't even have compartments on the walls, just a manual control panel on the other end that operated the bay doors.

Cass turned, facing the hallway once more. Where next? She touched her bracer to scroll available options on the HUD. Galleys, private cabins, bridge, wash rooms, maintenance rooms, laboratories. Laboratories? Yes, that would do it. There was *always* expensive shit in laboratories. Granted, sometimes selling them on the black market proved difficult, but not impossible. A narrower pool of buyers, sure, but still…

Cass made a left out of the cargo bay, careful not to make a sound. Her sister wasn't so careful, making just as much noise as she did on the *Trojan*. Cass glared over her shoulder at her, running a finger across her throat to ask for silence.

Jess ducked her head, shoulders hunched, and nodded.

Cass refocused on getting to the lab.

I wonder what they've got.

Kou had reached the bridge only to find more bodies slumped everywhere. The captain sat in his seat, head and upper body listing to the side. The navigator had cracked his forehead on the console when he'd passed out. Another person lay unconscious in the middle of the floor. He didn't bother trying to help any of them. It might seem cold, but the only way to help them was to get life support running again.

He frowned at the dark consoles. Almost everything was shut down, which was when he realized he couldn't feel the ship's engines through the floor. Usually, that gentle vibration served as a constant backdrop while in space, but it was gone now.

Which meant they were in serious trouble. The viewscreen was black, but it didn't matter. Without engines, without propulsion, they had no way of steering or slowing down. If *anything* was in their way, they would hit it.

"Why is this happening now?" Was he still paying for failing his unit so long ago? Why did his crew have to suffer for it?

Then he heard it, a voice. He froze, closing his eyes to focus. A second voice, this one different, deeper, almost husky. He liked the sound of it. He could imagine a voice like that whispering in his ear, inviting him to bed. Hacht. And with a voice like that, he would probably say yes.

But he didn't understand the words. It was a language he didn't recognize.

Invaders.

His hands twitched, going to the weapons in his shoulder holsters. He pulled them both out and leveled them at the bridge door.

Time to hunt.

They slipped into the laboratory without issue. *This is more like it.* Cass's head rotated, taking in the territory. Lab benches broke up the enormous space with larger equipment lining the walls. Black countertops commanded attention in contrast to the brightly colored emergency equipment. She walked gingerly through the space, avoiding broken glassware.

The place was a mess now, most of the lab in disarray or broken. Clearly, no one had expected *her*. She smirked, but kept searching. The equipment on the walls would fetch a pretty price, but they were heavy, hard to move with just the two of them. She preferred more mobile options.

Walking between the benches, she spotted a safe low on the back wall. Cass picked up her pace, glass crackling under her boots. She stopped and knelt, lifting her bracer, smiling when it said, "Unlock Safe." She could kiss the damn thing.

Cass tapped her bracer, and the little safe made the biggest, most horrendous sound, like a thousand bolts sliding against metal at once. She grimaced, grateful the crew wasn't awake to hear that. Inside, paperwork in folders sat on a narrow shelf at the top. She picked them up, leafing through the pages. Promising. Secrets could sell well, too. But she didn't know the language and put it back, hoping for something better.

"Oh, shiny," Jess said.

"Jess, rebreather, now!" she growled through her teeth, glaring at her little sister over her shoulder.

Jess rolled her eyes, but complied, dramatically putting the device back in place. She pointed at an object on the bottom shelf of the safe.

Cass looked down and saw why it had drawn Jess's attention. It was stunning. About the size of her fist, it was blue with black rock still crusted over it. But more than anything else, the blue rock glowed. She reached out her hand, wondering if she was being unendingly stupid by touching the luminescent blue rock without protection.

What was it? Why did it glow? She figured it probably had some significance if they were locking it away in a laboratory, but even if not, it would probably sell well for cosmetic reasons alone. Imagine making jewelry that glowed blue like that?

And she'd never seen anything like it before.

Yes, *this* was the score they'd been looking for. She picked it up and handed it to Jess so she could have her hands free. *Just in case.*

She motioned with a finger toward the door. Jess nodded and followed, their feet continuing to crunch over broken glass. Cass checked both ways at the door and headed back to the airlock. She smirked.

Another flawless job. Damn, she was good.

They were just approaching the airlock when the crack of boots on metal halted her. She glanced over her shoulder, eyes rounding as the giant from planetside ran at full speed toward them, one eye glowing as blue as the rock they'd stolen. "Shit," she said around her mouthpiece, the word unintelligible.

She grabbed Jess's arm and ran into the airlock, running as fast as she could. Her heart pounded in her chest, the thump thump of rushing blood the only sound she could hear.

Shit, shit, shit. How was he awake? How was he *running*?!

But it didn't matter as she slipped through the space, butting up against the interior door of the *Trojan*. She hit the controls with more urgency than grace, and the door slid open, spilling them into the ship. Jess fell to her knees, her rebreather spilling from her mouth and clacking to the floor. Cass spit her own out to the side, not noticing where it landed, and pulled both guns from their holsters. They resisted slightly, the stiff material almost entirely unused. "Don't move," she barked as she raised the guns, aiming them at the Ateles warrior.

He's not stopping. Oh God, he's not stopping.

Please don't make me shoot you.

CHAPTER THREE

*C*ass's hands trembled on the guns, the sight bobbing up and down between his chest and head.

Don't make me do this. Please don't make me do this.

Cass jerked as a sound blared and the interior door slid closed. He slammed against the door a moment later, banging his fists against the window. She glanced at Jess where her sister stood to the right of the door, her hand dropping from the panel. Jess shrugged, a shaky smile on her face.

Cass let out a sigh of relief, forgetting he could see her. Muffled shouts came from the airlock. "Go away!" she yelled.

Jess snorted. "Might help if you used the intercom." She pointed at the panel next to the door.

"Smartass." Cass stepped forward and holstered her guns, still a little shaky over having to draw them for the first time. She discretely took a deep breath and pressed the button on the top of the panel. "Please leave my airlock," she said in Usan. Most species seemed to speak Usan, the native tongue of the most annoyingly benevolent species known to man.

His head bobbed back and forth until he found the intercom controls inside the airlock. "Not until you return the package," he growled, his finger on the comm button.

Oooh, growly. Mama likey.

She looked over at Jess and the pretty rock her sister clutched to her chest, looking far too young and insecure. "Nah. It's shiny. I think I'll keep it."

"It's not yours!" He slammed against the window again.

Cass's eyes rounded as the door rattled slightly. Shit. Would the door hold? "Knock it off or I undock without closing the outer hatch!" It was an empty threat, but what else could she do?

He froze, hands still raised to beat on the window before glaring and dropping them to his sides.

"Better. Now, leave my ship."

"No." He glared, his frame going even more tense.

Damn, now what? She had no way of forcing him out, and she felt almost sick at the idea of leaving the hatch open when they detached. "Fine." She tapped the panel, closing the outer hatch, and walked away.

Jessie trailed her sister to the cockpit, constantly checking behind her. In her mind's eye, she kept seeing that man banging on the window, trapped in the airlock. She frowned as they entered, and Cass sat down.

"Angus, get us out of here."

"Aye, Captain."

She frowned, gripping her seatback, staring at the back of Cass's head. "Shouldn't we…"

Cass looked over her shoulder and glared. "Sit the fuck down, Jess."

"Cass!"

A clunk reverberated through the ship as they separated from their target.

Jessie sighed and sat down, but didn't buckle in. "Cass, what are we going to do with him? We can't leave him in there." She hated the whine in her voice as she spoke. Her sister still thought of her as a baby, whining didn't exactly help dispel that opinion.

"Not now, Jess."

"Then when?" This time, her voice was strong, and she wanted to wiggle at how badass she sounded, but that would defeat the image.

Jessie opened her mouth to continue her tirade, but Cass's expression when she looked at her shut her up. She looked tired, defeated, and something else she couldn't put a name to. She'd never seen that expression on her sister's face before. Cass was a badass, a pirate. She *took* what she needed from life and didn't need anyone's approval or permission. Jessie had always looked up to her, idolized her.

She looked away, hiding a smile. Cass had tried and failed to keep her from cursing, but again, she idolized Cass, cursing and all. Jessie had never understood why her older sister seemed so determined to keep her speech polite and appropriate. Cass was never appropriate and look where that got her. She had her own ship, two close friends, and had kept the two of them together despite the odds.

Jessie leaned forward in her seat and set her display to show the surveillance feed from the airlock. The big, black soldier leaning over, doing something at the wall. She squinted, not that it helped. Squinting wouldn't magically make the camera change to the perfect angle.

"Preparing to enter sub-space," Angus said over the speaker.

"What, you haven't done it already?" Cass snarked.

Then something slammed into them from behind. Jessie shrieked, spilling from the chair she'd only half been sitting in. Her knee banged against the console. "Fuck." It throbbed, and she rubbed at it, trying to work out the worst of the pain. *It'll probably bruise.* She was constantly bruising.

"What was that?" she said as she pulled herself to her feet, her knee not wanting to bend. *Maybe it's worse than I thought.* The last time her knee didn't want to bend, she'd taken off a layer of skin.

"Angus?" Cass barked, her knuckles going white as she gripped her armrests.

"We've been hit."

"No shit, Angus!"

Jessie sat and buckled in, not wanting a repeat performance. She checked her display. Their guest was lying on the ground, picking himself up slowly. Damn, it was not safe in there. "Maybe we should let him out."

"Not *now*, Jess. We have more important things to deal with." Cass turned to face Angus's speaker. "What hit us?"

"Large caliber physical ammunition."

Cass's face scrunched up in confusion. "What are you talking about? Aren't our shields designed for that?"

"Our shields are not fully tested with physical rounds due to a lack of military support during testing."

I didn't know that. Why did nobody tell her? She'd been living on this ship for years with her sister. She'd always thought the ship was safe, that they were protected, but they didn't know, did they?

"Shit," Cass said, shaking her head. She slammed her hand against her armrest. "Any damage?"

"Minor. The hit did not penetrate our hull."

"Are the shields fully operational?"

"They were not operational when the round hit. They are now."

Jessie followed the conversation back and forth, feeling completely useless. She didn't know how to use a gun, how to program. Hell, she didn't even know what questions to ask Angus in a situation like this. She glanced at her display again. Their guest had picked himself up now and had returned to the wall. Tension filled his frame, and he seemed more determined than ever at his task.

What was he *doing*?

Another hit jarred her in her seat, the force throwing off the ship's rotation and thus the artificial gravity. She gritted her teeth, grimacing as their guest slammed into a wall. They *really* needed to get him out of there. "I'm going to open the airlock inner doors." She reached for her console, but Cass smacked her hand away.

"Don't you dare, not while we're under attack. Are you insane?" She pointed toward the back of the ship. "That airlock is there for a reason! It's there to protect us. Opening that inner door in the middle of an attack is sheer madness."

"Well, what about him!" she yelled back, pointing at her display. "He's not safe in there."

"I know. There's nothing we can do yet. We have to focus on the problem at *hand*."

Jessie gritted her teeth and turned away. She had no argument against that and it chapped her hide. Why couldn't she come up with something? She peeked at the screen. He'd picked himself up again, his arms outstretched toward the walls, preparing for the next strike.

"Angus, get us out of here," Cass said.

"Entering sub-space."

Jessie's head popped up, not wanting to miss it. This was her favorite part of space travel. She loved the way the universe looked in sub-space. Everything became surreal and abstract, like a painting in a museum. She smiled in spite of the situation as space began to distort around them like a funhouse mirror.

She held her breath. Almost there.

———

Kou held onto the cold metal walls, bracing himself for another hit. These pirates were going to get him killed.

Or I am. I'm *the one who boarded their ship, after all.*

He frowned at his own self-deprecating logic, but he couldn't dispute it. He should have stayed with his crew, got the ship up and running again. Now, they would probably die, never knowing what had happened, never knowing they'd failed.

And it was his fault, yet again.

He clenched his fists against the walls and looked over at the control panel he'd managed to pry open. One corner bent out toward the room and wires spilled out above the hole. It had probably been the epitome of stupid to try to mess with the panel. He didn't know what the hacht he was doing and was just as likely to open the outer hatch as the inner.

But he had to try something. That package was *their* responsibility and because he was security on board, it was *his* responsibility to get it back. Seeing the little girl cradling it to her chest had shocked him. How did the pirates find it? The scientists had locked it away in the lab in anticipation of starting their experiments.

Not that he had any clue what those experiments entailed. Kou was the muscle, after all, the grunt. He didn't get included in those kinds of decisions. He just kept everyone safe.

Failed in that, too, didn't ya?

They took another hit, the ship rocking beneath him, but he was better braced this time. He shifted, but kept his feet.

Those two had better have a plan.

Suddenly, the sound of the engines changed. He'd never heard anything like it, and he froze, wondering what the hacht it could be. For a moment, time stood still, then a loud boom rocked the ship. He dropped to his knees as the new engine noise changed, sounding angry.

Something's about to break.

Kou tried to brace himself, laying flat on the floor and lacing his fingers over his neck to protect it. He counted the passage of time by his deep breaths. His pounding heartbeat mocked him, fighting against his efforts to stay calm. From the floor of the airlock, he couldn't tell what was happening. Were they still being pursued? Were they going to be stranded, idling in space? Would they crash?

Then the sound of the engine abruptly stopped, and Kou held his breath.

There was a moment when all was peaceful, quiet. He almost thought everything would be okay.

Then a red haze filled the room, and he looked up, realizing there was a window in the outer hatch.

They were entering atmosphere.

Hacht. He didn't think that was on purpose.

Kou dipped his head down again and tried to relax. He'd been through enough collisions, falls, and other injuries to know to relax. He breathed deep once more, focusing on his muscles, on releasing the tension there. Wind howled just outside the walls, but he pushed it from his mind.

We're going to die.

He pushed the thought away. It wouldn't help.

We're going to crash.

His jaw tensed, but he forced himself to relax it.

Clear your mind. Relax.

The howling grew until he imagined malevolent spirits screaming to be let in. They would scratch at the door, their terrifying voices piercing the brain, tormenting those who dared to listen.

Then the ride was over, the ship slamming into the ground. For a moment, it felt like his body was almost weightless as screeching metal filled his ears. Then his body slammed into something hard, and he roared as his right leg plowed into the floor.

But it didn't end there. He lost count of the times a body part banged into something or screamed out in pain. He couldn't quite process what he was seeing, hearing, or feeling.

Then the back of his head exploded in pain, his neck contorting forward, and the world ended.

CHAPTER FOUR

*C*ass breathed heavily as she sat strapped in her seat, gripping the harness. Every muscle hurt from tensing during the crash. She couldn't believe it, her mind skipping over the reality.

They'd crashed. They'd actually fucking crashed.

When Angus reported they were entering sub-space, she thought they'd made it, that they would outrun their pursuers. She'd never heard of any other species that used sub-space, which meant they couldn't follow. It took special engines to do so, and humans weren't the best at sharing.

As she tried to get her breathing under control, a looping replay of the crash played out in her head.

Reality distorted in the viewscreen as they started to enter sub-space, but then an explosion rocked the ship. Jess screamed, her voice piercing, but almost drowned out by the chaos.

Cass wanted to tell her it would be okay, that they would be fine, but she couldn't find her voice.

Then they finished entering sub-space. But even she *could tell the engines didn't sound right. "Status report," she barked at Angus, but her voice didn't carry above a whisper.*

It didn't matter, anyway. A moment later, Angus's voice cut through the air. "Critical engine failure imminent. Taking us out of sub-space."

Jess's scream renewed.

"Give me a sitrep," Cass yelled. This time, her voice carried.

"Unknown. Analyzing."

Shit.

She waited, her breath shaking, but she didn't have long to wait. As soon as they exited sub-space, with a new solar system surrounding them, the engines cut out, deafening silence prevailing.

"Angus!" she yelled, panic sending her body into chaos.

I'm not like this. I don't panic. I have to stay in control.

But she wasn't *in control.*

A planet loomed in front of them, and she didn't even register its appearance before their viewscreen flared red as they became caught in the planet's gravity well.

"Angus, slow us down."

"Trying. We have auxiliary thrusters and reverse thrusters, but we've lost the sub-space drive and the primary ion propulsion engines."

"English, Angus!"

"I canna guarantee a safe landing."

Translation: We're going to crash.

She gripped tighter to her straps, trying to calm her breathing. Closing her eyes, she prayed for salvation she knew *wouldn't come.*

Faith can't save you.

Cass just hoped Vicky's safety features did the trick. She didn't know what they were, but she knew they were there.

"Oh, God," Jess cried from beside her.

She opened her eyes. Terrain was flying past below them.

Too fast. Too close.

The ship screeched and groaned as they clipped the top of a mountain, the nose bouncing up after impact. For a moment, she couldn't see the ground, just clear, almost green sky.

Then the nose dipped down once more and they started skimming the tree tops, the branches whipping past the viewscreen.

Too fast.

Then time suspended. Jess wasn't screaming, Cass's heart wasn't pounding, and she could no longer hear the wind roaring around their ship. Trees filled the viewscreen, simple and majestic. She couldn't tell much about them other than they, too, were green.

Then the nose dipped once more, angling directly for the forest below. Unholy cracks echoed around them, and the viewscreen went black. The cameras must have broken on impact, but the ship was still moving.

Her anxiety rose, not knowing what lay ahead driving her half mad. What was happening out there? They were still going so damned fast. How could they possibly survive?

Then the Trojan *slammed hard, shuddering and groaning with the impact, but it didn't stop. They jerked in their seats, but the harnesses held them steady. The ship bounced up again, slamming hard into the ground over and over as the insane speeds of space travel continued to carry them forward, ripping through the landscape she couldn't see.*

How are we not dead yet?

Then they hit the ground one final time. This time, instead of bouncing, they skidded, the ship spinning a little as it came to a halt.

Cass let out another slow breath, trying to push the nightmare from her mind. Her chest hurt. She unclasped her harness and pulled her shirt aside at the neck. Black bruises covered her shoulder where her harness had held her in place. It disappeared under her clothing, and she bet she would be sporting bruises everywhere.

She looked over at her sister, who was whimpering in her seat. "Jess, you okay? Speak to me, all right?"

"Hurts." Her voice barely carried.

"I know. That's the price of living. But we're alive. We survived the crash. That's the important part, okay?"

Jess nodded.

Cass stood, kneeling in front of her little sister, palpating up her arms, checking for broken bones. She continued on, checking collarbones, ribs.

"Stop it, I'm fine," Jess said, trying to squirm out of her reach, but the harness kept her in place.

Cass smiled. "You're fine, eh?" Then she proceeded to tickle her ribs.

Jess squealed, her legs kicking wildly as she squirmed in her seat, trying to escape Cass's devilish fingers. "Mercy, mercy!"

Cass laughed, pulling back. "I think you're fine."

Jess rolled her eyes. "Didn't I *say* so?"

"Yes, you did." She looked around the cockpit, really seeing it for the first time since they stopped moving. Lights flickered in the ceiling and the room looked alarmingly dark. "Angus, sitrep," she said. Her voice sounded tired and a little raw.

"Still analyzing. So far, I have received no structural integrity alarms, though sensors *could* be damaged. I am deploying bots to scan the outer hull."

"Do we have comms?"

"Unknown. We are currently not sustaining sufficient power for a consistent communications signal."

"Not even TAT?"

"No, not even TAT. Last known locations for both Victoria and Eleanor are too close for a low power TAT signal without breaking causality."

"Damn." She stood, banging her fist against the console.

"Easy, sis," Jess said as she popped her buckle, throwing the straps over her head. "We don't need any *more* damage."

Cass sighed. This was a nightmare. "How long until we know the full extent of the damage?"

"A few hours, at least," Angus said.

Cass nodded. Until they had a full report on the ship's status, they couldn't do much. And until they had comms, they could do almost nothing. She just *knew* they would need parts to repair the sub-space drive and primary propulsion engines. For that, they needed Vicky.

"What about the alien?" Jess said, touching her shoulder.

Cass spun around. "The what?"

"The alien? In the airlock?"

Cass froze. She'd completely forgotten about him. Damn. What was wrong with her? She turned to Jess, but her sister wasn't looking at her. She'd turned to the display beside her, which was actually still working.

"Oh my God!" Jess's hands went up to her mouth. "He's not moving! Is he dead?"

Cass came up behind her sister and wrapped her in a hug. "Don't borrow trouble," she said, checking the screen herself. He lay on the ground, motionless, but the camera didn't give enough detail to tell if he was still breathing. "Schrödinger's Cat. Remember that? Until we get there, he could be alive or dead. There's no point worrying about it until we get there."

Jess nodded. "Okay."

Kou lay on the ground, staring up at the ceiling. He wanted to say the floor was hard or cold. He wanted to say he was in agonizing pain, but he wasn't, which was so much worse. Sweet Atala, he couldn't feel a thing.

He knew what that meant. He'd broken his spine, damaged his spinal cord. It wasn't unexpected. The Ateles were prone to spinal cord injuries because they moved just as efficiently on four limbs as on two. Unfortunately, creatures that moved on four legs tended to have their skulls attached differently than bipeds. The necessary flexibility of their necks to accommodate that difference meant spinal injuries were common.

It's why they developed the Nanotechnology that coursed through his body to begin with, the Nanotechnology that saved him, turned him into a cyborg. Generations ago, a spinal injury might as well have been a death sentence. They couldn't treat it, couldn't repair it. But nanos could bridge the broken connection, restore the link between brain and body.

It was that thought alone that kept him from going insane. He just had to wait, be patient. He had to let the nanos do their work, corrupt him even further than they already had so many years ago.

Then the airlock's inner door opened, heralded by the sound of the metal sliding into place in the wall. Boots clapped against the floor and he twisted his eyes painfully to the side to try to see. It was them, wasn't it? The thieves.

A wash of purple hair fluttered in the corner of his vision before hovering above him.

They spoke back and forth in a language he couldn't understand. The small one, the child, sounded alarmed while the adult female remained calm. She kneeled next to him. He could see her knees pressing into his side, but he couldn't feel it, not the pressure, not the heat.

She pushed her hair out of her face with one hand, touching his chest gently with the other as she leaned over him. She looked into his eyes, searching for something. "Can you speak?" she asked in Usan.

He wanted to say yes, but his body wouldn't cooperate. Her face scrunched up. She turned to the child and spoke, pointing through the door.

The little girl nodded and dashed out, disappearing out of sight with an unbearable racket. The woman turned back to him, patting him on the chest. "You're going to be okay. We'll take good care of you."

Something in her gaze seemed so sincere, though he didn't know her species at all, didn't know their mannerisms. For all he knew, her species used expressions like that to draw in prey.

Cass sat on her knees, the metal floor digging in, making her want to move, but she resisted. The heat of his body seeped into her from her contact with his side and it felt good. The only person she'd touched lately was her sister, and it wasn't the same.

Of course, this wasn't either. The man was injured. She was no medic, no doctor, but even *she* could see that. He needed help and didn't seem able to move.

Think, damn it.

She needed to immobilize his neck. She'd sent Jess to get their emergency kit, which *should* include everything to stabilize a person. Where *was* that kid? She stared through the door, leaning farther over to try to see, but nothing. "Jess?"

"Coming," she said, but Cass still didn't hear her sister's obnoxiously loud footsteps.

"This isn't leisure time. Get your ass moving," she yelled.

"I said I'm coming already. *God.*" Finally, Jess's steps rang through the hall, heralding her approach.

Cass turned back to her patient, not knowing what to do. They had a medical suite, complete with automated diagnostics systems, but they were intended for humans or shifters. Ellie had some Ateles soldiers on her ship now, but Cass hadn't gotten around to updating the software yet.

She forced a smile, trying to be reassuring. She might hate that he'd stolen aboard her ship, but she wasn't heartless.

"God, why do we have so much shit," her sister said from the doorway, dropping the kit next to Cass.

She turned to face her. "Because it's far better to have it and not need it than need it and not have it. We lead dangerous lives, Jess."

Jess sighed. "I know."

Cass unzipped the red and black bag, pulling the seam apart. First, she grabbed the neck stabilizer and wrapped it around his neck. He stared at her the entire time, his gaze intense. For a moment, she couldn't look away, captured as she was.

Then she shook herself and examined the rest of him. Other than being motionless, he looked fine—no blood, no tears—until she reached his leg. There, the leg bent at an angle that didn't match his other leg.

Broken bone. Open fracture.

They would need to be careful with that.

She turned back to the bag and unstrapped the portable stretcher. Sliding the bag out of the way, she rested the compact stretcher near his head and pressed the button. It extended to its full length, which didn't quite reach his feet.

She frowned. That wouldn't do. They would need to stabilize his broken leg before they could carry him back to medical. She scooted over to the bag again, pulling out an inflatable cast. She stretched it out and laid it next to his leg before looking him in the eyes. "This'll probably hurt."

He gave no sign he understood. She sighed and waved Jess over. "I'm going to lift his leg. You get the cast underneath."

"Sure thing."

They worked in tandem. Once the clear plastic cast rested under his leg, Cass lowered his limb, then secured the buckle straps and snapped the inner coin that caused the cast to inflate.

He didn't make a noise.

She checked him again, but he didn't seem any different from before. He didn't respond at all, which worried her. There was no telling what happened to him in this airlock while they crashed. Cass and Jess had been strapped in, and even *they* hadn't been completely unaffected. She rubbed a sore spot on her chest.

"Jess, help me get him on the stretcher."

"How the hell are we gonna do that? He must weigh a thousand pounds!"

"Jess!" she snapped at her sister, exasperated with her attitude. They didn't have time for this. They'd crash landed on an unknown planet. They didn't know if the planet was hospitable, if the ship was intact, if they could get comms up, or if they could get back in space.

As she looked down at her patient, she realized they didn't even know if the diagnostics system would work. Practically nothing else did.

Cass returned to the head of the stretcher, figuring that part of him would be heaviest. "I'm going to lift his shoulder. You push the stretcher under him."

"Fine," Jess said, rolling her eyes.

Cass shook her head. How had she not killed the teenager by now? She settled her fingers under the bulk of his shoulder, registering the hard metal underneath his shirt. She froze, surprised, and looked at his face once more, noting the metal that covered half his face. The material continued down his neck, disappearing beneath his collar. How far did it go?

It didn't matter. What mattered was getting him on the stretcher. She lifted with all her weight, but his shoulders wanted to curl in on themselves, causing most of his back to remain on the ground. "Come on, fucker." She shifted her right hand farther back, pushing up on his right shoulder blade.

Jess pushed the stretcher in place. The narrow rod bumped against his opposite shoulder before Cass eased him back down, the backs of her hands scraping against the rough canvas that connected the two poles. She looked at them, the skin raw and chapped.

Shaking them out, she stood, straddling his hips, and squatted, lifting with her knees. "Again."

Jess complied, the edge of the stretcher popping out the other side.

Cass stepped over his inert body, going to his feet, where she carefully settled them on the stretcher. Now, his feet and a single arm and shoulder hung off the edges. She returned to his head and shuffled him until he was on there properly. She looked up at Jess. "Now we just need to carry him to medical."

Jess scoffed. "Good luck with that."

"Come on, brat. You can take his feet." Cass waited until Jess got into place, but while Jess had no problem getting his feet off the ground, Cass felt like she was trying to lift a truck. "Fuck." She let go, shaking out her hands.

She frowned. It was no use. She couldn't lift him, not like that. Good thing she was a shifter. It gave her unparalleled control over her body. She could spike her adrenaline to insane levels or even redistribute body mass. "This is gonna suck." As her adrenaline spiked, she picked up the stretcher. This time, while it strained her muscles, she could lift him. "Let's go, Jess."

"Yes, ma'am."

The ship wasn't terribly big, so it didn't take more than a minute or two to reach medical. After they dropped him on the scanner bed, she flexed her hands, the fingers and palms sore to the touch. "Damn."

Now they just needed to get him squared away before the adrenaline crash hit. "Angus, start the scan."

"I cannot guarantee the results."

"Well, will it hurt him?"

"Nay."

She crossed her arms under her breasts. "Then do it."

"Aye, Captain."

As the automated diagnostic system hummed to life, it didn't resemble in any way the stuff of Sci-Fi movies. There wasn't a holographic display hovering over his body. In fact, it would be easy to think nothing was happening.

"Missing diagnostic reference data for species: Ateles," Angus said a few moments later.

"Well, what the hell can you do?" she yelled.

"Based on best estimates of the alien's physiology, I've identified a probable break in his right leg and another in the cervical vertebrae."

"Can they be fixed?"

"My automated systems can fix the leg fracture, but its unclear the severity of the vertebral fracture."

"Meaning?"

"Based on lack of movement, spinal cord integrity is questionable."

She looked down at him. He was paralyzed? Shit. "How can we know for sure?"

"Look in the top drawer on the right."

Cass crossed the room, opening the drawer. "Now what?"

"Take a syringe and stab his fingertips."

"What?" Her hand dropped from the drawer, a little horrified. "Why the hell?"

"Most sentient species should have sensitive fingertips for dexterity purposes."

"Right," she grumbled, fisting the syringe angrily and returning to the patient's side. "Sorry about this." She looked at him, but he just looked resigned. Trying to be even a little gentle, she pressed the sharp tip into the meaty part of his finger. There wasn't so much as a tremor as she pressed it almost to the bone and removed it again. "He didn't feel that. He didn't feel that at all."

What were they going to do with him?

"He may recover without intervention." Angus's brogue broke the silence.

"What? How is that possible? He's paralyzed, for fuck's sake!" Cass threw up her hands, frustrated with how fucked up everything had gotten so damned fast.

"Some Ateles are injected with nanotechnology capable of reparative work. Based on this individual's appearance, I believe he has those in his system."

She looked down at him, wondering what Angus saw that she didn't. "What about his appearance?"

"He's a cyborg."

"So?" She glanced back, noting all the metal on his face and neck. Did that make him a cyborg? She'd never met one before, had only heard of them in fiction.

"Ateles cyborgs should all have the nanotechnology active in their bodies."

Right. How the hell did Angus know this shit? She'd programed him, and even *she* didn't know where he got some of the stuff he'd learned.

Feeling sorry for him, she reached out and held the injured man's hand, lifting it so he could see because he couldn't feel it. He should know he wasn't alone, that she would be there for him. For now.

"Do what you can for him, Angus."

"Aye, Captain."

<hr>

Kou woke up in the thief's medical facility. It had been surreal knowing they were fixing his broken leg, but not being able to feel or even see it. This time, the woman sat in a chair by his bed, her legs propped up by his hip as she focused on a tablet in her lap.

His body tingled, like pins and needles, everywhere. It was reassuring, if painful. Still, he couldn't move.

You'll be better soon.

The reassurance didn't help much. How could it when he lay there hopeless, helpless, at the mercy of a thief who'd likely killed his entire crew?

But then why did she help him? Why not just dump him out of the airlock?

Then he remembered that moment as he raced to reach her before the airlock closed. She'd stood there, poised with her weapons raised. There had been several moments there where she could have shot him. Nothing more than squeezing a finger; that was all it would have taken to end his life. But she'd hesitated. In that moment, he couldn't read her expression, didn't know what it meant, and he still agonized over it, wondering what she'd been thinking when she spared his life.

Why did you do it?

Why did you spare me?

Would he ever get an answer?

He tried again to move, even something so little as a single finger.

Nothing.

<hr>

Cass was only half reading. Usually Chad Sexington had her undivided attention, but not today, not with the Ateles male laying still as death beside her. For hours now, the only movement from him had been the rise and fall of his chest as he breathed.

It probably didn't help that she'd been fighting an adrenaline crash that wanted her to curl up in her chair and sleep, either. And it was easy to forget when tired that she could control her hormones, snap herself out of it.

With a deep breath, she turned to her patient, a dark, forbidding slab of muscle stretched out on the medical bed like an inanimate object. "Maybe I should read to you," she said, resting her tablet in her lap. "Though I'm not sure how much you'd enjoy the sexcapades of Chad Sexington. Then again, the book's in English, so maybe you wouldn't care.

"Angus says you'll probably recover, which I think is pretty amazing. I'm a shifter, so I know what it's like to recover from the seemingly impossible, but it's still scary." She looked at him more critically, wondering what he was thinking. "I imagine this must be terrifying right now. I know I would hate it."

Cass ran her hand over the edge of the tablet, watching and waiting for even the smallest twitch to indicate he was improving.

"Maybe I will read to you. It'll pass the time, at least."

She started reading slowly, trying to translate the book into Usan as she went. It was slow, having to figure out the words sentence by sentence, but it kept her distracted and maybe it did the same for him.

Hours passed that way, lost in the story, until a growly voice broke the spell, the rolling tones reminding her of a Scottish brogue, only more foreign.

"What the hacht are you reading?"

CHAPTER FIVE

Kou tried to push himself into a sitting position, but his muscles trembled from resting so long. He glared at the woman by his bed. The pins and needles sensation had abated, but his body felt weak as a newborn babe.

He'd wondered earlier what she was reading, but now he wished he hadn't found out. Usan certainly wasn't his native tongue, but the writing she'd been reading him had been atrocious. And he wasn't one to read often.

"Easy, bud. It'll take a little bit to get your strength back." She stood, pressing on his chest to push him back onto the bed. "Don't worry. You'll be back on your feet before you know it."

"Where's the package?" he snarled.

She gave him a look he took to be disgruntled. "What package?"

He tried to lean up once more, but it was futile. Her single hand was enough to keep his weak form flat on his back. "What you stole."

She crossed her arms. "I'm not telling you. It's none of your business, anyway. It's mine now."

He growled. "It's *not* yours. You stole it. Return it *now!*"

"No!" she barked back, placing her face so close to his own he could feel her hot, humid breath fanning over his face.

"Yes! It's not yours, and you have no idea the hacht you have brought down on your shoulders."

That gave her pause. She pulled back. "What do you mean?"

And then the child burst into the room.

<hr>

"What the hell, Cass? How can you pick a fight with an invalid?!" Jess said, throwing her hands up in the air.

Cass turned and glared at her little sister. "He started it." She was immediately ashamed of the words that came out of her mouth. Really? He started it? She snapped her mouth shut.

"Oh, he's moving." Jess stalled out in surprise. "When did this happen?"

Cass shrugged. "Just now."

Jess rolled her eyes. "You couldn't wait more than a few seconds to pick a fight with him, now could you?"

Cass stepped back and dropped into her seat. "And you're surprised?"

Jess shook her head. "No, nothing surprises me about you anymore."

"Thanks, brat," she said sarcastically.

"Hey, no problem." She stepped farther into the room. "So, do you think he'll be up and about soon?"

"How would I know? I'm not a doctor."

Jess shrugged and plopped down on the edge of the bed. She turned to the patient. "Hi, my name's Jessie. What's yours?"

Cass shook her head. "I'm pretty sure he doesn't speak English, Jess."

"Oh, right. Let's see." She scratched her chin. Jess rarely had to speak Usan, so it didn't come to her as easily as it did Cass. "Hello. My name is Jessie. What is yours?"

He stared at her little sister like she was some strange creature he had yet to figure out. "Kou," he said finally.

"Oooh." Jess wiggled in place with her excitement. "Kou is cool. Our friend's boyfriend is like you, only with less metal." She tapped his left cheek, and he flinched.

Cass sighed. "Jess, don't touch people without their permission."

Jess raised an eyebrow. "And what have *you* been doing since the crash?"

Cass crossed her arms. "Responding to emergencies."

"And that's an excuse?"

"Knock it off, Jess."

Jess huffed, facing away in a snit.

Cass stood again, ignoring her sister. She would get over it, eventually. As she loomed over Kou, she remembered what Jess had interrupted. "What did you mean?"

"What?" he rasped.

"What do you know about the crash? About the attack?" What was his crew *up* to?

"You stole something of grave significance."

Cass waved her hand in the air. "Yeah, yeah. Get to the juicy parts."

He frowned at her.

She leaned in. "Stop being so damn vague."

"The people that shot at you are willing to kill to get the package you stole."

She leaned back, scoffing. "Do you think I'm an idiot? Give me something I can actually *work* with!" Her impotence and defenselessness ate at her as she hovered over him. She wanted to shake him, but it wasn't his fault the ship had crashed. Of all things, she couldn't lay *that* at his feet.

"There's not much I can tell you. I had countless files on our ship's computers, but I don't have access to them now."

"Well, is it a government, business, what?"

"It's a business. They've managed to keep out of the jurisdiction of each government by keeping themselves off the grid. They build space stations away from any claimed solar system so they can make their own rules. They have more money than most governments and the militia to back up anything they wish to enforce."

She sighed. "Great." She ran her hand through her hair. "What's their MO?"

"Their what?"

"Their modus operandi."

"I have no idea what that is."

Of course, he didn't. It was Latin, for fuck's sake. He didn't know English. Why would he know that? "What type of tactics do they usually use to reach an end goal?"

"Whatever it takes. They have no MO, as you call it. If a single ship can accomplish it, that's what they'll do. Or a military. Or a bounty. They will do and pay whatever it takes if they are sufficiently motivated."

Cass scratched her chin. "Pay whatever it takes, eh?"

Kou jerked up, pointing a shaking finger in her face. "Don't you dare." His voice was dark, dangerous. She liked it.

Cass shrugged. "What do I care who buys it? If they'll pay good money to retrieve it, they can pay *me* that money. Not like I care who pays."

"It's not theirs!" he roared.

"So the fuck what!" she yelled back, leaning into his face.

He collapsed to the bed's surface in defeat. "Just don't. Please don't."

Cass walked out of medical, leaving Jess to watch after Kou. His words, his plea kept getting to her as she walked down the hall, looking for a little distance, looking for a little privacy.

Standing in the entry to the cockpit, she was struck by a sense of helplessness. Where usually she would see a picture of space, there was now only darkness. It matched her mood.

"What do I do?" She'd always lived her life with a strong sense of the path forward, even when that path sucked. If she continued as she always had, she would sell the damn rock to the highest bidder and get the hell out of Dodge.

But then his words would ring through her head, making her question her path, her sanity.

"Angus?" she said plaintively, feeling like a little girl.

"Aye, Captain?"

She sniffed, surprised that her eyes felt moist. "What's our status?"

"I haven't finished my full analysis, however we will not be able to repair the engines without synthesizing parts."

Shit.

"I cannot complete a full scan of remaining systems without repairing the generators. Based on the information I've collected, you should be able to perform the repairs with my guidance."

"What about the bots?" She appreciated the distraction, but the bots were designed for that type of work, and Angus guided them directly. They could probably accomplish it in a fraction of the time.

"They are currently inspecting the hull for compromise."

"Still?"

"Aye. They have provided data on 76% of the hull."

"Right, never mind. Lead the way."

Kou stared, alarmed, as Cass left the room. He wanted to chase after her, try to convince her not to sell the package, but even sitting up left his entire body trembling.

Hacht.

He couldn't let her sell it. He might just be a grunt, but he knew enough about the material to know it couldn't get in the wrong hands. And the Diehli were definitely the wrong hands.

But what could he do? She was as stubborn as the goddess herself. Ordinarily, he liked that in a woman, but now wasn't the time. He *needed* to make her see.

And he needed to check on his crew. If the atmospherics didn't drop too low, and the Diehli didn't attack, they might still be okay. It was a long shot, but he didn't want to think of the alternative.

"So, Kou," the child said, a sly smile on her face.

He frowned, not sure what to make of the girl. She was small, frail, but with the first blooms of womanhood, at least based on the woman's example. They appeared to be the same species.

She reached out, running a finger over his chin where metal met fur. Then she leaned in, pushing her arms together so they plumped her young breasts.

His frown grew, and he leaned back, trying to retrieve some personal space from the little girl.

But she wasn't having it. She scooted even closer, resting her hand on his thigh. He froze, shocked that a child would even do such a thing.

She doesn't know what she's doing.

It means nothing.

He lightly gripped her hand, reseating it on her lap, and held out a hand, indicating she should step back.

She stuck out her lower lip, her shoulders hunching slightly. "But Kou…"

How the hacht did he get in *this mess?*

Cass leaned in, trying to make sense of the wires before her. "I'm going to kill Angus," she grumbled. She couldn't keep them straight, having come close to clipping or crossing the wrong wires three times now.

I have no business doing this.

But there was no one else, so it had to be her. Why couldn't it have been a software glitch? She could handle a software issue in her sleep, but with this she was all thumbs.

"Ow. Damn it." She jerked away, sticking her cut finger in her mouth.

She leaned back, staring at the open electrical panel. One of the strikes had hit the engines, causing most of the damage. Unfortunately, that same strike had caused an electrical surge from the engines to the generators, causing fried circuits and wiring everywhere. Angus was on a separate system, so he was in good shape, but almost everything else relied on the generators.

She sighed, feeling like they would never get off the ground again.

"Cass?"

She spun around, cut finger still in her mouth. "Kou," she said, the single syllable muffled. She pulled the digit out. "What are you doing here?"

He looked around, looking a little lost. "I…"

Cass stood. "How are you up and about?"

"After a short nap, I'm feeling a lot stronger. Almost back to normal."

Cass frowned, not sure if she should believe him. She didn't know the Ateles culture very well, but if they were anything like human men, they didn't like to admit weakness.

She shooed him toward the exit. "Come on. Maybe you should head back to bed, just in case."

"No, I'm fine," he said, his body becoming an immovable object.

"I guess you are. I can't push you around anymore." She smiled at him, remembering how hot she'd always found Zee. She ran a hand up and down his arm, admiring the muscle definition. It was his right arm, and it had just enough give to assure her it was all muscle, but damn if it wasn't nearly as hard as the left.

"Cass?" He looked down at her, surprised.

She stepped back, cocking her head. "What? I like how you look. You look like you'd be a good fuck."

"We've done nothing but fight."

She shrugged. "So? Sometimes that's even better." She leaned in and traced the muscles on his chest.

Different.

For a moment, she was fascinated by the novel lines and angles, determined to learn each one.

Kou grabbed her wrist, pulling her hand back. He bent down, looking into her eyes. "You can't sell that package."

Cass ripped her hand away. "Says who?" She pointed her finger in his face. "I can do whatever the fuck I want. And there's not a damn thing you or anyone else can say about it." She shoved him with both hands, but of course, he didn't budge.

Damn cyborg.

Angus interrupted their unproductive bitch match. "Cass, we have a problem."

CHAPTER SIX

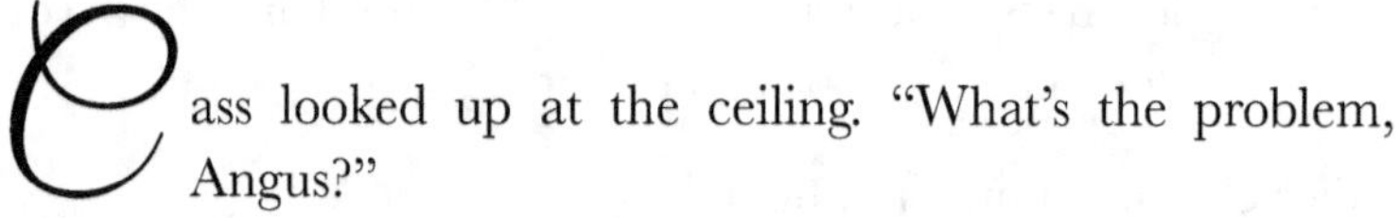

ass looked up at the ceiling. "What's the problem, Angus?"

"Food and water systems are out of order."

"What the hell does that mean?"

"The ship canna filter or pump any more water. We have stores of food, however, refrigeration units are currently offline. I would advise not opening any sub zero units until power is restored."

Shit.

Unlike in Earth homes, ships required power to pump water. They might have filtered water in a tank somewhere, but what good did it do them if they couldn't get to it?

"So leave the freezer alone, eat all the refrigerated stuff, and we need to hunt for water. Do we know if it's safe outside?"

"Aye. I've already scanned the surrounding environment for necessary oxygen content as well as airborne toxins and microbes. It seems safe."

She hated that phrase, "seems safe." Really, it translated to, "I tried, but you may die anyway."

Cass ran her hand through her hair and shook her head, not liking her options. They could use a portable gravity-fed filtration system to get drinkable water from local sources. It wasn't a perfect solution, and they all might get a bit stinky, but it was their best option. She sighed. "Well, we've got no choice. Angus, have you been able to run a scan for bodies of water?"

"Aye, Captain, I'll link it to your bracer."

"Thanks, Angus." She put down her tools and turned to Kou. "You should head back to medical. You're too weak for this excursion." She left the room without looking back, heading for the cargo bay. She'd already geared up before she spun around and bumped into Kou. "Jesus Christ, Kou. What the fuck?"

"I'm coming with you." He crossed his arms over his chest, looking both sexy and menacing at the same time.

Should be a sin.

"Listen, Chad Sexington." She poked his chest.

"What? My name is Kou."

She shook her head. "Not the point. You just recovered from being *paralyzed.* You should be recuperating, not gallivanting across an alien world."

"I do not need to recuperate. I need to stretch my limbs, work my muscles."

"In a controlled environment!" She pointed away from him. "If you exhaust yourself out there, I can't save you." She pointed at herself this time. "You're too damn heavy and that's *far* too much distance. God only knows how far we need to go."

"I'm coming and that's final," he growled, leaning forward so their noses nearly touched.

"Fine." She threw up both hands. "It's your funeral." She pointed at him one final time. "But I am *not* carrying you back here. If you can't make it back on your own, you're dying on this fucking planet. Got me?"

"I don't quite understand the phrase, but yes."

She rolled her eyes. "Whatever," she whispered and took off.

<hr>

The sun warmed Kou's skin and seared his sensitive eyes as he followed Cass off the ship. He chastised himself for letting his ego, his pride, get the better of him. He'd *planned* to search the ship for the package when he'd stumbled upon her. Then when she'd insinuated he was weak, that he couldn't hold his own, he'd snapped, blinded to the task at hand.

It was beyond stupid, and he couldn't believe he'd fallen for the trap. But then, she seemed to have a knack for throwing him off his guard. Like when she started hitting on him. How could she just go from screaming her head off at him to wanting him? It made no sense.

There had to be an ulterior motive, but what? *She* had the package. She certainly didn't need him for anything, unless she hoped to gain information about the Diehli so she could sell it to them. He shuddered, horrified at the thought of those gangsters getting their hands on it.

How did they even find out about it? He'd been careful, obsessive really, about mission security. He always was. But they still found out, still attacked. What was their game plan? If Cass hadn't struck first, what would they have done? More importantly, what would they do now?

Could they track her ship? He didn't know her technology, didn't know if the ship had any stealth capabilities or special engines that could aid her in losing them. Could the Diehli be bearing down on them right now while they were stranded?

He reached for his weapons, nestled snugly in their holsters. They'd removed his guns, but it hadn't taken him more than a few moments with the child's back turned to find them. The solid weight comforted him, reassuring him he wasn't completely defenseless.

Not like after the crash.

That was one of the worst moments of his life, laying there, unable to move, unable to fight back. She could have raised her weapon and shot him between the eyes, and he couldn't have done anything to stop her.

And yet she didn't. Over and over again, he'd found himself at her mercy, and she hesitated. Was it that she *couldn't* pull the trigger or didn't want to?

It didn't matter. It didn't matter if she had a heart of gold and couldn't hurt an animal, let alone a person. He had to retrieve the package and return to his crew. That was the only option.

He couldn't give into her.

He just couldn't.

***

"Kou, where the hell did you go? You're supposed to be in bed!" Jessie yelled as she stood in the doorway of medical. Only silence answered. "Angus! Where is everyone?" She was surprised Cass hadn't barked at her by now for making a racket.

"Kou and the captain have left to collect water."

She frowned. "Why would they do that? There's water on the ship."

"The water pumps and filtration systems are out of order."

"Great." Just what they needed. "Any other surprises, Angus?"

"Not at the moment."

Jessie leaned against the wall, staring at her murals. "What should I do? What is there *to* do?" She was *supposed* to be checking up on Kou, but he left with Cass.

She always gets the guys.

What *was* it about her older sister? Guys came crawling to her like she was an oasis in the middle of a desert. It made no sense. Her own awkward self couldn't tempt a man trapped in his own sick bed.

Maybe it was because she was trans. You wouldn't know it from looking at her, but she was assigned male at birth. Could they just sense it, like a predator senses prey? Was she never going to feel like a real girl? In her head, she was. Physically, she was, but what did that matter if people didn't treat her that way.

Cass had treated her like a girl from the day she announced she was one. Not a batted eye, not a single question. Just, "Okay," and they moved on with their lives. Ellie and Victoria were good about it, too. Ellie knew about her insecurities and always tried to make her feel better about herself. And Victoria was too absorbed in her work to even notice.

But that was okay. Victoria was cool. She built this ship, designed it from scratch. It didn't get much cooler than that. Jessie loved this ship. It was home, and she never wanted to leave.

She pushed off the wall and wandered to the cargo bay. She didn't really want to be alone in her room right now and she wasn't hungry, so the galley had no appeal, either. As she entered, her gaze latched onto the smuggler's hold where she'd hidden the rock they stole.

He'd been so insistent they return it.

She'd never really thought about the right and wrong of what they did for a living. What did it matter? The universe was a harsh, unforgiving place. It just seemed logical to take what you needed.

Well, at least, that was what Cass always said. Somehow, it had never seemed all that harsh and unforgiving to her. Cass was the only family she ever knew, ever had. And she might be rough around the edges, but she was like a momma bear. She would do anything to protect her cub.

And she had, hadn't she? There were times growing up she rarely saw Cass. She didn't understand at first. When she was so little, all she understood was no one was there. She would cry, screaming for her mother, a mother who would never come. A mother who'd abandoned her before Jessie had even formed memories of her.

Jessie rubbed her neck, feeling uncomfortable reliving those memories. Those were times in her life she would gladly forget.

Letting out a sigh, she looked around the cargo bay. Knowing Cass, there was bound to be *something* out of order, something to put to rights. She walked up to the gear wall. There were big gaps in the equipment.

That's right. Cass and Kou went outside.

But there was also stuff from their hijacking just thrown up against the wall. She picked up Cass's bulletproof jacket, running her fingers over the coarse material, before hanging it up and securing it with straps. Everything had to have straps because of their work. They always lost gravity when they docked.

Jessie checked the straps and compartments, making sure everything was secure. "This sucks."

Cass walked through the forest. She wasn't much into wilderness. She'd had enough of *that* living with the shifter caravan. Even so, a wave of nostalgia hit her as she traveled through the dense foliage. It reminded her of living in the caravan, living off the land. There weren't a lot of places on Earth this lush anymore. And the vegetation reminded her of the tiny oasis they'd created in a messy, ugly world.

Looking up, light filtered through the canopy, turning the leaves into shining emeralds. The ground was packed earth, and the bark looked scorched, like a recent forest fire had cleared out the underbrush.

"Over here," she said, following her HUD. A red flashing outline lit up the display, making her think of a river or stream. She couldn't tell which.

Cass picked up speed, jogging, her boots kicking up dust around her.

The trees started to thin, and she leaned into her momentum, ready to *be* there already. She was so *damn* impatient, but she'd accepted that about herself long ago and had learned to run with it. She burst out of the tree line, skidding to a stop as the hard dirt turned to rocks and sand that shifted under her, making her footing precarious.

Looking over her shoulder, she smirked at Kou, who was jogging sedately and shaking his head at her.

"Don't ruin my fun, Chad Sexington."

"My name is Kou."

"Details." She turned back to the water. It moved lazily, and the current tempted her to strip and jump in, enjoy a good swim. After all, they wouldn't have any running water for a while. Might as well.

Duty first.

She pulled the rolled-up collapsible jugs from her pockets and bent over the water's edge, careful not to let the tiny waves lap against her boots. One after the next, she filled the two jugs and capped them for transport. They were going to be a bitch to carry, but there was no helping that. The walk back was just going to suck.

Finished with her task, she looked around, spotting Kou just a few feet upstream, his second jug almost full as well.

Cass stood up, walking toward him. She leaned against his back as he crouched, and he jumped, sloshing water over his hand.

"So, now that the work is done, how about we play?"

Kou spun and grabbed her hand, pulling her away from him. "I'm not *playing* with you."

She pouted strategically, though it didn't seem to have the desired effect on him. "I just thought we could go for a swim," she said, running a finger over her neckline suggestively.

"I don't think that's a good idea." He looked away, grabbing his jugs to walk away.

She latched onto his arm. "You're not going to leave me to swim on my own, are you? That's not safe."

He paused, and she smirked. *Gotcha.*

He sighed. "Very well, but I'm not joining you." He placed the jugs down and crossed his arms.

She smiled at him, faking gratitude when, really, she was feeling gleeful with success. "Thank you." Then she proceeded to strip very, very slowly. She ran her hands over her body as she shucked each garment, folding and setting them down neatly on her boots so she could wiggle her ass in his face the entire time.

When she turned back, he looked alarmed. "I'm going in now." But as her gaze dipped down, she noticed a formidable bulge. He wasn't *completely* unaffected.

The water lapped cool against her ankles as she dipped her toes in the water. The wet sand squished between her toes, and she turned to face him. "Are you sure you don't want to join me?" She continued to touch herself in nonsexual places, but the slow rhythm suggested everything she wanted to do to him.

His face darkened, if that were possible with the naturally dark complexion of an Ateles, and his stance stiffened. "I'm sure."

She shrugged. "Your loss." She backed into the water, the line of the water's surface sliding up her calves, her thighs, until her hips were submerged. She ran her hands over the surface, enjoying the gentle feel as it played with her sensitive skin.

Near the middle now, she doubted the water would get much deeper, so she let her feet drift from the bottom. She started swimming and floating, but kept her front facing the surface so

Kou had a view. "Are you *sure* you don't want to come?" She smirked at her double entendre.

"I'm *sure.*" He sounded strained.

"Pity. I'd love to see you come."

He choked, and she looked away, hiding her smile at his expense. He might be a tough nut to crack, but by damn, she would crack him.

Then something brushed against her leg. She dropped her feet to the ground, but didn't see anything in the water in front of her. She turned, looking behind her. Nothing.

It brushed her inner thigh. She jumped. *Calm down, Cass. It's probably just a fish.*

Still, she was naked, and it made her feel vulnerable. With Kou, she felt in control, on the hunt, but the unknown something in the water made her feel unsettled.

"Is everything all right?" Kou asked, concern in his rough voice.

"Yeah. Felt something in the water."

"Maybe you should come out now."

Yeah, right. She had a stubborn streak a mile wide. "It's fine." She didn't really feel like swimming, and she probably wouldn't be able to seduce Kou now that she'd made him concerned for her, but she didn't like being forced to call it quits. "Just a little longer, and I'll come out."

Cass dived in, the water cold against her face as she submerged fully for the first time. She kicked out and something rammed against her between her legs. She shrieked, water pouring into her mouth. Her arms flailed as she shoved up toward the surface, the pressure still intense between her legs. She coughed, slapping the water as she tried to get her feet under her.

There was something between her legs and, oh God, it was pushing into her. "Get it out!" she shrieked. She reached between her legs, trying to get a hold of it, but couldn't get traction. Oh God, it was going deeper. And it was big, too big. And long.

Then it stopped. Cass panted where she stood in the water, her legs spread wide as she continued to whimper in panic. She reached down, her hands trembling, but there was nothing to grab. She could feel the smooth surface of the end of it stretching her open. God, how big was it? Now that her brain was clearing, it hurt. It felt like her insides were burning.

What the hell just happened?

Kou stood there shocked as Cass surged from the water, sputtering and flailing. She was screeching in her native tongue as he ran into the water. His soaked clothes clung to him as each movement caused water to splash up around him, soaking him further. His boots, now waterlogged, became sluggish, slowing him down as much as the water did, but he finally reached her.

Pulling her into his arms, he uttered soothing sounds, sounds his mother once made to him when he cried as a child. "Calm down." He rubbed her strangely smooth back.

Tears streamed down her face as she looked up at him. She'd grown silent, but now she started to beg, again, this time in a plaintive tone that melted his heart a little.

"Please speak in Usan. I can't understand you." He caressed her face with his other hand.

"Please get it out." Her voice trembled. She looked and sounded pitiful.

It surprised him. He'd enjoyed her stubbornness and strength even while it frustrated him. He'd never expected to see a side like this to her. It left him defenseless against her and, unlike last time, he didn't mind this so much. "Get what out? Where is it?"

She pointed between them to her nether regions.

He looked down, surprised. "Okay." He lifted her out of the water, resting her on the sandy shore. "Let's see what we're working with." Her legs flopped open, and he immediately suspected the problem.

Something big and black currently stretched what he assumed was her reproductive hole. Red, almost angry lips surrounded it, stretched wide around the object with tufts of hair on the outer edges. "I'm going to try to grab it."

She nodded, her face red and puffy.

He reached out, running his fingertips around the edge of her hole, working them in around the object. When his fingers were in and he could grip it, he pulled.

She shrieked. "Stop, stop! It hurts!"

He froze. It hadn't even budged.

What the hell was it?

CHAPTER SEVEN

fter her first attempts to walk back under her own steam, which resulted in her feet beyond shoulder-width apart, Kou had grunted, putting his jugs of water down on the beach and lifting her into his arms.

"Kou, no!" She'd smacked at him, his arm stinging from the impact.

But he wasn't having any of that. "Stop. You can't walk. This will be faster. We need to get you back to medical to run a scan. Don't you want that thing removed as fast as possible?"

She'd nodded and shut her mouth, burrowing her face against his chest.

Now at medical, he placed her gently on the scanning bed. "Angus, run a scan," he said, remembering the name they'd used when working on him.

"Aye, sir," the AI replied.

It surprised him. He'd half expected the AI to snub him since he wasn't a member of the crew. Apparently, it didn't have those types of security protocols.

"Scan complete."

"What is it, Angus?" Cass said, her voice shaky.

"Based on the basal morphology, I postulate it is a hecto-cotylus."

"A what?" she jerked up, flinching and falling back to the bed.

"A hectocotylus is the reproductive limb of some varieties of aquatic species."

"It's a dick?" She paused as if to let that sink in. "There's a dick stuck in me?"

"Not quite, but yes."

"Then how come we can't remove it?" Kou stepped forward, suddenly feeling a little protective of Cass.

"According to scans, this particular species utilizes barbs to prevent removal. In theory, it would increase the probability of mating success and reduces competition."

"It can't be removed? What the fuck?"

She jerked in place and Kou pressed on her chest, keeping her from hurting herself again.

"Unknown. I will have to do additional research."

"What?" Cass jerked against his hand.

I should just keep my hand here. She can't seem to sit still.

"How long?" Kou asked, resigned to keeping her out of trouble in the meantime.

"Unknown. I don't have sufficient information at this time."

"Oh, fuck me." She banged her head against the bed.

"I think something already has."

Cass glared at him, and he lifted his hands in surrender.

Cass was so frustrated. And she couldn't even be angry at Kou for his comment. It was mean, but it was also a bit funny. If she weren't in such a funk.

Stuck on the bed in medical, there wasn't much to look at except a plain, metal ceiling and Kou's fantastic, muscly form. Unfortunately, her current predicament made her less than enthusiastic about the normally titillating latter option.

How could things have gone so wrong? *Years* of flawless jobs, of successful flirtations with practically every species she'd ever met, and yet nothing had gone right since she started this mess.

Her ship was fucked up, they had an unwanted guest who wanted her hard-earned loot back, she'd failed epically at seducing him, and now the wrong dick was stuck inside her.

She ran a hand through her hair, tugging at the strands as she thought. The sharp sting helped clear her mind. Could she do some shape-shifting to remove the thing? She frowned, doubting that would work. Of course, if she tore herself, it didn't take long for a shifter to heal.

Problem is, I'm a pansy when it comes to pain.

Nobody knew that one. She kept that secret locked down tight. No one needed to know the badass Cass was really just posturing.

Her mind's eye returned to that moment in the hall, her shaking guns trained on Kou. She couldn't do it. She couldn't pull the triggers. How could she call herself a pirate when she couldn't even kill someone? She used subterfuge and computer programs to steal. She had all the swagger, but her spine was a wet noodle.

"Cass!" Jess yelled, her voice bouncing off the walls.

Cass gripped Kou's arm, having a hard time getting a hand-hold. "Please, don't let her see me like this."

Jessie jumped as a commotion rang out behind her. She pivoted on her heels. "Should they be back yet?" She turned to the gear wall in the cargo bay, staring at the pistols lined up, all neat and tidy. What if it wasn't her sister? What if an animal had snuck in? It could be dangerous.

She reached up, squeezing the grip as she unfastened a gun from the wall. It felt heavy and cold. The textured grip was foreign in her tiny hands, making her feel even more the imposter. Her sister had never trained her on its use. Could she even fire it? Did she dare?

She checked its black surface, familiarizing herself with the design. *Where's the safety?* She planned to keep the safety *on*, but it paid to know where it was. An image popped into her head of a predator bearing down on her while the gun click, click, clicked in her hand.

She shook the image off. This wasn't like her. She wasn't the pessimistic one. That was her sister. *Jessie* was the one who thought Kou shouldn't be left in the airlock. And she'd been right. He wouldn't have broken his neck if they'd secured him before crashing.

As she lifted the weapon, keeping it close to her body because her thin arms just wouldn't hold it out straight without shaking, she treaded carefully to the side entrance where the commotion had occurred.

She tried to be quiet, but she had no practice in it. Her shoes echoed off the walls, making her wince. Well, she'd already announced herself… "Hello?"

Jessie peeked around the corner. The door to the outside was open, but there was nothing in sight. The hallway was quiet, and out the door, trees swayed gently in the breeze, their leaves rustling.

She swallowed hard, anxiety growing. "Angus?" she whispered.

"Aye, Jessie." Angus didn't bother to be quiet. That must mean there was nothing to fear.

"Who just entered the ship?"

"The captain and Kou."

She nodded. "Where are they?"

"Medical."

Jessie froze in place, gun clutched to her chest. "Medical?" She dropped the gun from her nerveless hands and dashed off, the weapon clanging against the metal floor plates behind her.

Shit.

What happened?

Cass…

"Cass!" Her feet clamored on the floor tiles, making her wish for the thousandth time that they had something other than metal beneath their feet.

She skidded to a halt as Kou stepped into the hall right outside medical. She tried to move around him, but he shifted in place, blocking her. "What the hell, Kou! Let me see my sister!"

"No." He crossed his arms, his face taking on the stern expression Zee made from time to time.

"What the fuck!" she cried out, shoving him with both hands, but he might as well have been a brick wall. He didn't move an inch. "Move!" She tried to move around him, but he was a wily one, simply taking a step back so his frame eclipsed the entire doorway.

"Ah!" she screamed in frustration. She stomped her foot and tore off for her room. When she slammed the door behind her, her rage evaporated. She slammed her back against the door and slipped to the floor where she'd added soft floor covering.

The entire room was a riot of color. The floor had a rainbow of different carpet colors, each a separate square so they could still access the maintenance space beneath. She'd painted the walls herself, much like she had in the hallway. Only here, she'd done so at an earlier age. She'd been fascinated with unicorns at the time, so unicorns and rainbows covered the walls. She'd outgrown that stage in her life, but couldn't bring herself to paint over them. "This is a part of my childhood."

And for that reason alone, she couldn't bring herself to eradicate it. She could no more do that than she could throw away her countless drawings, some of which she'd taped to the white spaces on the walls. It made the room crowded, chaotic, but alive with color, with life.

"Cass." She couldn't forget about Cass. Was she okay? Why was Kou blocking her from the room? What if she was dead? She gasped, covering her mouth to hold in a sob.

"No." She shook her head. No, it couldn't be.

She pushed herself to her feet. "Drawing will help." Jessie always lost herself in her drawing. She crossed the room to her desk and scooped her pad and pencils out of the drawer, dropping to sit on the bed, back against the wall. She pulled up her knees, propping the drawing pad on her thighs and let her hand move freely over the paper. It didn't matter what she created.

She just needed to bleed onto the page.

After the little girl stomped off in a huff, Kou turned and reentered the room. "Angus, is there anything we can do?" In the center of medical, Cass lay on the exam bed, looking resigned and miserable. He felt for her and crossed the room, sitting in the chair close by.

"I have narrowed down possible worlds based on planetary characteristics and our known trajectories when we crashed. Currently running a search of databases for likely species."

Kou gripped Cass's hand, returning the favor for when she did this for him. At the time, he couldn't feel anything, but knowing someone was there for him had been huge, even if she *was* the enemy. It had kept him sane.

With little she could do other than talking, he tried to wrack his brain for a safe topic, one that wouldn't start an argument. "So, how did you end up in space?"

She turned her head on the bed's pillow, just looking at him for several moments before speaking. "Our friend, Vicky. She built these ships." Cass looked toward the ceiling again, a smirk stretching her lips. "She wasn't very good at programming, though. When she got to a certain stage with her first ship, she asked for my help. I developed Angus and programs to run and monitor the systems.

"It was good seeing her building her ships." Her smile grew. "She was so passionate. In the evenings, when she finally finished working, she would sit in the main tent and talk about spaceship design while members of the caravan circled around her in rapt attention." She shook her head and laughed. "I suspect she would have been just as happy talking to Timmy."

"Who's Timmy?"

"This little robot hobbled together by one of the men in the camp. The thing was a monstrosity… and really obnoxious, but he'd made it when he was a teenager, and he had a certain sentimental attachment to it.

"Anyway, for whatever reason, she didn't stop at one ship. I've always wondered why. I knew she was struggling. Vicky moved in with us when she was sixteen, but the apartment we were living in was a terrible environment for her. She wasn't getting better. She was the reason we moved to the caravan. I'd hoped the quieter, calmer life might suit her better, that being around fewer people might help, too. On some level, I always wondered if her obsession with spaceships masked a deep-seated desire to run away.

"But she waited to run until we all could. I don't think she ever expected I'd…" She paused, looking over at Kou apprehensively. "Anyway, how did you end up on *your* crew?" she said, changing the subject.

He suspected he knew why. He suspected she'd been about to mention piracy, then thought better of it. Kou was willing to allow the subject change, but how much was he really willing to talk on the new subject? "I was military."

"I figured."

He nodded, trying to control the urge to cover his left side. The military had given him a mental health discharge shortly after the injuries that had taken so much from him. For a time, he'd gone to therapy, but therapy had only seemed to highlight the flaws he saw in himself, encouraging him to examine them and get some perspective.

It hadn't worked.

Though the military paid for the sessions, he quit after less than a year, feeling more broken than when he started. He'd spent time barely leaving his small apartment in the capital city of Ateel, getting everything he needed delivered. He had exercise equipment there and routinely worked himself to exhaustion, hoping the exertion would quiet his crippling mind.

But he couldn't tell her that. He couldn't tell her how broken he was, how Captain Welgan offering him a position on his crew had been an essential lifeline, pulling him out of the depths of his own darkness. They'd worked on many jobs together before the one that led to him meeting Cass. In that time, he'd built back his confidence piece by piece and proved himself a capable member of the crew, even if he questioned his own decisions constantly.

He took a deep breath and said what he was comfortable saying. "After the military, I was offered a position on the ship you found me on. I'd worked there for several years before the current mission."

"Did you like it?"

Did he? His mind drew a blank at her question. He didn't know. It had been a job, a purpose, when he had none. It had been a way to drag himself out of his own self-loathing. Did he like it? Did it matter? He shrugged, feeling uncomfortable voicing the truth.

"Yeah, I get how that is," she said. "Before I left Earth, I was always working for someone else. Sometimes, it was a toxic environment, boys' clubs when those types of antics were illegal. Other times, it was just long, hard hours and crappy pay.

It was never really rewarding and usually wasn't enough to keep food on the table. I learned to program at an early age, but I started cracking because I couldn't let my sister down. When I looked at her, I knew I would do anything for her."

Kou had never had anything like that in his life, except maybe the soldiers in his unit… and they were all gone now.

Because of him.

Cass yawned, drawing him out of another dark spiral.

"You should get some rest. I'm not going anywhere," he whispered to her as she nodded and closed her eyes.

Cass woke to Angus's brogue on the intercom. "I have identified the species."

"About damn time," she grumbled, rubbing the sleep from her eyes, her vision red behind her eyelids.

Beside her, Kou gave her a bemused look.

"What?" she said, glaring at him.

"Nothing." Yet he smiled at her.

Weirdo.

"According to the research data I accessed, it is, in fact, a hectocotylus."

"English, Angus."

"We're speaking Usan."

Cass banged her head against the bed. "You know what I mean!"

"Aye."

"Wait," she said, lifting onto her elbows carefully. "How do you have all this data?"

A pregnant pause settled over the room and if Angus could have a physical form, it would have been that of a pre-adolescent boy squirming under his mother's censure. "After the incident with Ellie's ship, I decided to download databases of information I thought I might need in case of another communications blackout."

Cass sighed. She couldn't really blame him. Angus was accustomed to having access to whatever information he needed at the drop of a hat. It wouldn't sit well with him going blind. "Is that why the search took so long?" It had been hours. In that time, she'd almost gotten used to the "hectocotylus" stretching her inner muscles.

"Aye," he said, his tone dejected. "My databases are a bit… bloated. I need to reindex them."

She nodded. "So, what's the situation?"

"It'll take a couple hours to run an indexing protocol."

"*Not* what I meant, Angus."

"Aye, of course. Well, the barbs will retract on their own."

"When?"

"Unclear. The research data indicates a length of time, however I do not have a frame of reference for that unit of measure."

She sighed. "Great. Now what?"

"I'll run a scan every fifteen minutes to check if the barbs have retracted."

She banged her head against the bed once more.

"The barbs have retracted," Angus said over the intercom.

Kou looked up. Cass was asleep. She'd drifted off only a few diceros ago, and he didn't want to wake her.

But she sure as hacht doesn't want that thing in her any longer than necessary.

He agonized over the situation for a few more moments, then shrugged. She *had* asked him to remove it before. It should be fine. She still wasn't wearing pants, so he spread her legs and settled his elbows on the middle of the bed between them. Again, he could see the black end of the hectocotylus spreading her wide.

He reached out, working his fingers around the object. This time, he didn't have Cass's panic infecting him and he paused, distracted by the feel of her. She was warm and damp, her soft skin caressing his fingertips. His dick twitched in response, taking the act as an invitation for playtime regardless of what his head said.

You're an Atala-cursed reprobate, Kou.

But the inner scolding did nothing for the state of his loins. They didn't care that he was performing what equated to a medical procedure on her. They didn't care that she wouldn't welcome him taking advantage of the situation.

Yes, she would. His brain taunted him, completely without honor. *She was practically begging for it earlier.*

He shook his head, ashamed of himself. But Sweet Atala, she felt nice. He could spend an evening in bed with her, just lazily running a finger over her silken skin.

Hacht me. Stop it!

Kou took in a deep breath, wondering when he'd become such a pervert. He slipped his fingers in a little deeper, getting a good hold on the object, and pulled gently. This time, she didn't scream. This time, it slipped out just as easily as his own member would.

When it came out all the way, her hole quivered as it tried to adjust to not being filled. He stared down at the object. It was like nothing he'd ever seen. Certainly, they didn't have anything like it on Ateles. While roughly the size of his own cock, it had floppy appendages around it and he could see where the barbs had retracted, now tiny holes marking the surface.

He dropped it in the nearby trash disposal unit, wiping his hands on his pants. But as he lifted his hand closer to his face, he could still smell her on his flesh, faint but tantalizing.

What was *wrong* with him?

"I am detecting unidentified technology on my active scans," Angus said, breaking into Kou's thoughts.

Someone's here.

CHAPTER EIGHT

Cass woke as Kou stuck his fingers in her. She looked down as he paused, a pained expression on his face as his body tensed between her spread knees. Damn, but she wished it was *him* inside her and not that *thing.* She bet they would have a mighty good time.

His fingers flexed, and she kept quiet and still as he pulled it out, her muscles aching around it. She tried to keep her heavy breathing quiet as she recovered, resisting the urge to press her legs together. Really, that would just mean wrapping them around Kou with where he was positioned. She smiled. It was a good mental image.

Then Angus spoke up, sending a splash of cold water over her hormones. She sat up quickly but winced as discomfort rushed through her. She still hadn't recovered. Didn't have time to recover, really. "Angus, what are you detecting?" she barked as her bare feet slapped against the flooring. "Kou, where's my pants?"

He started handing her clothing, looking a little surprised, and she suspected, embarrassed.

"Not now," she whispered to him as she pulled the pants over her waist and grabbed her boots, not bothering with securing anything. "Heading to the bridge, Angus."

She walked gingerly at first, and Kou took her arm, guiding her along. She swallowed her pride, her knee-jerk reaction being to bite his head off. After all, it was a sweet, if ill-placed, gesture.

"Angus, what do we know?" she barked at the ceiling as they moved.

"Still collecting data."

She stopped, shifting in place to relieve the discomfort. "Then why did you tell us?"

"I thought you should be informed."

Cass hung her head, wondering where she'd gone wrong in his programming. "Tell us what you *do* know." She continued to the cockpit, taking her time as she dropped carefully to her seat.

"A few moments ago, my active scans detected the presence of refined materials."

"Metal?"

"Unclear. The scan was unable to acquire consistent data."

Kou stepped forward, a dark mass creeping into her peripheral vision. "Do you think it was cloaked?"

"That is a possible scenario."

Cass ran her fingers through her hair, thinking. "That would be a glitch, though, with a cloaking system. How many systems are vulnerable to that type of glitch?"

"I'll run a database search."

Cass sighed. "Well, this'll take a while."

Kou gripped her shoulder, massaging the muscle there. "Have a little faith."

She scoffed. "Faith can't save you."

Kou's hand froze on her shoulder, but he didn't say anything, for which she was grateful. She didn't want to have that argument with him. From the experiences they'd had thus far, she could only imagine how *that* would go.

<hr>

Kou had followed Cass to the cockpit as the AI hedged on the details of his discovery. He remained tense as they waited, trying not to think about how tragic it was for such a young woman to be so pessimistic, so jaded.

Faith can't save you.

That one statement probably revealed more about her than she realized, and it made him wonder just what had happened in her short life to make her feel so.

Cass tilted her head back to look at him, speaking out of the blue. "Why is it so important to you that I return the rock, that it doesn't get into the wrong hands?"

Kou was startled by the question, not expecting it. So far, she had blasted him with her determination to sell it, regardless of the buyer. To have her listen to his side of things took him aback. He swallowed hard. "Well, I'm not one of the scientists, so I can't say I know all the details."

She waved her hand around. "Yeah, I understand. Go on."

"I know it was recently discovered, and they were very excited about it. They planned to study it, learn its properties so they could develop scans to find more of it."

She turned around in her seat, gripping its back. "What makes it so special?"

He didn't rightly know. They often talked about how it was groundbreaking, revolutionary, but then they would start going on and on about loads and units of measure he'd never heard of before. "I'm… not sure." He shook his head, frustrated with himself. "They believed the signature would be identifiable from a distance."

"From a distance? Signature?" Her gaze became distant before she shook her head. "There's only one thing I can think of that could be *that* significant and easy to scan for."

"What's that?"

"A new energy source."

"You mean like for powering ships?"

She lifted her shoulders. "Or even cities. If it's what I think it is, there's no telling how much power it can output, but considering your buddies went to an awful lot of trouble to get it…"

"They're not my buddies!"

She raised up her hands. "I was referring to your crew… but the bastards who shot us out of the sky count, too."

He glared, but didn't comment.

She leaned back, looking at him thoughtfully.

What was she thinking?

***

Cass was chagrined, churning with indecision as she paced her bedroom, kicking piles of clothes out of her path. She didn't want to admit it, even to herself, but she was starting to rethink her stance.

Which just fucking pissed her off. She was a pirate, for fuck's sake! Pirates steal. That's their job. They don't go giving shit back to their rightful owners. That would be utter mayhem.

And she certainly didn't feel bad about it, not at all. If they didn't want their shit stolen, they should have secured it better, as far as she was concerned.

But then why did Kou's words leave her thinking so goddamned much? Why did she keep running them over and over in her head? He didn't mean anything to her, and she certainly didn't trust him. She didn't trust anyone. She didn't. He was just someone she wanted to bang.

Badly.

Cass frowned and dropped down on the end of her bed, the surface bouncing her up and down before settling. She'd never let her hormones fuck with her better judgment before. And giving back the thrice-cursed rock without seeing a dime for it would definitely be against her better judgment.

So why? Why couldn't she get it out of her head? Why couldn't she let it go?

But she didn't get to work that out because Angus disrupted her thoughts. "Update. Confirmed: ship detected. It matches the parameters of the ship that attacked us."

"Shit," she said, jumping to her feet. She paced back and forth, frustrated and just a bit scared.

What do I do?

CHAPTER NINE

Jessie put her drawing pad down, staring at the replica of Kou. She ran a finger along the glass-slick surface of the pad's screen. In the picture, he gave a devilish smile and winked. She shook her head. She didn't know why she'd chosen to draw him like that, but it made her feel a little better.

And she'd needed that. This mission had left her self-esteem in tatters in spite of her sister allowing her to accompany her onto the target ship for the first time. *That* had been exciting. But getting shot down by Kou? Not so much.

She thought about that big body hidden behind that gray uniform, and her face heated. She ducked her head, embarrassed even though no one could see her. He'd rejected her. Her sister had the hots for him. Why couldn't she let it go?

Sitting on the bed, running her hands over the soft comforter, she was tempted to just stay in her room until he left or she died of embarrassment, whichever came first. But that would be the coward's way out, and her sister didn't raise a coward.

She pushed off the bed, her heavy boots muffled by the carpet on the floor. "I'm not a coward." Saying it out loud, she almost believed it. She shook her arms out, trying to release the tension that lingered there, and walked out of her room.

At the door, she looked down the hallway in each direction. The hall was empty, but she could hear voices in the cockpit to her left. She followed the sound, the words becoming more distinct as she approached.

They were speaking in Usan, so she had to focus to eavesdrop.

"What are your strategic advantages?" Kou asked, his voice so authoritative, it made her shiver.

"Strategic advantages?" Cass laughed, her throaty voice like a goddess in the small space. "What strategic advantages? Almost all of our systems are down. Even if they weren't, at best, we've got a pulse weapon. That's it."

Jessie grew closer as the conversation paused. *What's going on?*

"You're a pirate, yet you have no weapons, no shields?"

Cass scoffed, the sound thick in her throat. "Hardly. The shields don't operate in an atmosphere with flammable gases. Or they do, but it's dangerous as hell. And I just said we have a pulse weapon. Useful, but again, nothing's working."

Jessie stepped into the cockpit. Neither Kou nor Cass had even noticed her as she came to a stop in the doorway.

"There is currently insufficient power to activate either the pulse weapon or the shields as the repairs have not been completed," Angus chimed in over the speakers.

"Thanks," Cass said dryly. "Way to shove me under the bus."

"What?" Kou said, his face scrunching up in confusion.

"What the hell is going on?" Jessie said.

Kou jumped at the child's exclamation. He'd been deep in thought, worrying about how to protect the ship and keep the package out of enemy hands. Sure, he might not like the situation he was in, begging a pirate to do the right thing, but the Diehli served as a far greater threat. Fortunately, he was starting to suspect that Cass was becoming just as wary of the Diehli as he was.

"We need to form a strategy." He'd never had to protect an asset with so few resources before. He wasn't sure what was the best path forward. "What other resources do we have for when they find us?"

"We have weapons and armor in the cargo bay. Not military grade, but functional."

Kou paused to stare at her. She was fierce, defensive of her equipment, like she expected him to judge her. "We can't defend ourselves if they use their ship, so we have to ensure they need to land and continue on foot."

She ran a hand through her hair, the short purple strands clinging to her neck and struggling to curve around the arc of her ear. "I don't think they *can* strike from the ship, not without risking the package."

He shook himself, prying his mind from the erotic picture she presented. "They did before."

"True, but they might not have realized we had it."

Kou's gut churned ominously. He hadn't thought of that. Did they board Captain Welgan's ship? What would the Diehli have done with the crew? Were they dead? Had he failed yet again? He'd been so focused on retrieving the package that he'd barely thought about his crew. In some part of his mind, he'd just assumed they would be fine, but if the Diehli had already been there? That hope seemed deluded now.

"I suppose whether they knew then is a non-issue. They followed us here. We have to assume they know now."

"And blowing us up won't get them the rock."

"No, it won't." He rubbed his chin. "They'll either have to raid the ship or have us come to them."

"And we'll be ready for them."

Cass felt numb as she sat in the cockpit, staring at the blank display after her meeting with the others. She needed to get her shit together, but how could she possibly pull off her normal bullshit bravado right now? She certainly didn't feel it. If anything, she felt nauseous. The most responsibility she'd ever had was taking care of her little sister, and that had often been overwhelming.

But this? This was just too much. She was a small fish swimming with sharks, and she feared she was about to be eaten. Cass wanted to be rational about this, look at the data and come to her own conclusion, but the stakes were so damn high, she couldn't even fully grasp what she was dealing with. She was relying on information given to her by others. How could she possibly make the right decision?

And when the hell did she start trying to do what was right? She was a pirate, for Christ's sake! And why did she suddenly have to keep reminding herself of that? She'd never questioned her direction in life, not once. She wouldn't say she was a good person. If anything, there was probably something seriously wrong with her morals. But even if she was having a midlife crisis, it didn't matter. What mattered was the threat approaching. What mattered was protecting her family, protecting her ship.

Which just brought her right back to the problem at hand. What the hell was she going to do? She thought of trying to deal with the Diehli, the bastards Kou seemed so hell-bent against her selling the rock to. But frankly, she couldn't see that ending well. She wasn't operating from a position of strength. Their ship was damaged, they were probably outnumbered, and they couldn't reach out and request a meet in a public place.

All in all, any one of those things would make her hesitant about a meeting. And further, she liked to research her potential buyers and middlemen before meeting them. She liked knowing who she was dealing with and how to approach the negotiation. Nothing about this situation left her feeling confident.

Then a loud speaker blared, jarring her out of her never-ending thoughts. "Turn over the crystal or face destruction." The words almost reverberated through the space, freezing her in place.

That did it. Her indecision evaporated like so much fog.

CHAPTER TEN

ou was worried.

The exterior doors had been left open because of the repair efforts, allowing a Diehli drone to enter and broadcast a threat. Kou had left for the galley after their strategy session, but he'd rushed out when those ominous words had roared through the ship at full volume. He'd entered the hallway just in time to see Cass flinging a well-aimed knife into the drone's body. It dropped like a rock, its broken form sparking on the floor in its death throes as its propellers twitched and finally stopped.

When Cass stepped over the drone, she seemed entirely too calm, her body relaxed and face devoid of any expression he could recognize. He didn't trust that composure. He hadn't known her long, but Cass just didn't seem like that type of person. It made him think she was up to something, and that made him very nervous about the imminent future.

"Cass?" he said as she walked past.

But she ignored him. He followed her cautiously as she walked down the colorful hallway toward the cargo bay, but inside, tension ramped him up, leaving his mind a shambles. What was she up to? Did he need to stop her? Could he? Would he? Given the opportunity, he was starting to wonder if he had it in him anymore. She'd wheedled herself inside, and he wasn't sure he wanted to get her out.

But what if she betrayed him? What if she gave the package to them? Could he ever truly forgive her?

He was afraid to know the answer to that. He was afraid he wouldn't like what it said about him.

Kou stared at the back of her bright purple head as she geared up, preparing for battle. He'd been in the military long enough to recognize the process. She loaded up thigh holsters, boot sheaths, shoulder holsters. She donned bulletproof gear and various electronics. As she proceeded, clangs rang through the room as she not-too-gently grabbed gear off the wall.

Did all this preparation mean she was going to fight, that she wasn't going to give the rock up? Or was she gearing up as a show of force, as a way to show she meant business? Kou knew so little about her, about her business strategies and negotiating tactics. He hated that he didn't know. It left him flailing, unable to decide if he could trust her. She was a pirate, after all. Could they ever truly be trusted?

Does it matter?

Kou rested his hands against the hard metal of his own guns. One way or another, he needed to ensure that package didn't get into the wrong hands.

Jessie steamed as Cass and Kou walked off without even noticing her. Seriously? Like seriously! Was she invisible or something? She stormed after them, determined to give them a piece of her mind. As she reached the doorway to the cargo bay, her older sister was walking up to the gear wall.

With a huff, she stepped up to Cass. "I'm coming, too," she insisted, fists on hips.

Cass rounded on her, sticking a finger in her face. "Oh, fuck no, you're not." Her body was tense, and she had a look of cool determination Jessie had never seen before on her face.

"Cass!" Jessie screeched as she stomped her foot.

"No. I am *not* letting you go out there with an unknown threat looming."

Jessie huffed, but tried to get herself under control, taking a deep breath. "You let me in on the heist," she reminded her sister.

"That was different. There shouldn't have been any danger there." Cass turned back to the gear wall, as if the conversation was over.

"And there will be this time?" she said, incredulous.

"Yes," Kou said from behind her.

"Butt out of it, shit for brains," she said, pointing an accusing finger at him. She didn't need him ganging up on her, too.

He lifted his hands, and she turned back to her sister, who stood unmoving.

Now, Jessie was genuinely worried. *Would* it be dangerous this time? She didn't want her sister going into danger. She wanted Cass here, safe.

"Don't go." Her lower lip quivered as she looked up into Cass's blue eyes. "Don't leave me here," she said as she shook her head.

Cass gripped her by the shoulders. "I have to. Don't worry. I'll be fine. You just stay here, on the ship. I'll be back before you know it." She touched Jessie's cheek, causing tears to well up. "I need you safe, okay?"

Jessie nodded, but she felt gutted. "I need you safe, too."

Cass laughed and playfully messed up Jessie's hair. "I know, kiddo. I've done this countless times, haven't I? I've always come back. This isn't gonna be any different."

But this *was* different. Jessie could feel it.

Would her sister be able to keep her promise?

Would she come back?

Or would Jessie lose everything?

Cass stormed forward after grabbing the rest of her gear, a wave of determination driving her onward. A chaotic swirl of emotions tried to drown her, but she pushed them down. She'd tried to reassure her sister, but she'd lied. She *knew* this was different, that she might not come back.

Don't think about it.

And yet, she didn't want to focus on the plan, either. Her hand reached behind her, touching the paper-wrapped "package" strapped to her lower back. She paused for a moment on the ramp, her feet angled downward as nature played its music chaotically around her.

She glanced over her shoulder at Kou, but quickly looked away. He looked disappointed, and it gutted her.

This is necessary.

We have no choice.

But that didn't make her path any easier. She advanced across the hard-packed earth, stepping into the tree line. Before she'd killed it with a knife, the drone had told them to meet in a clearing not far from their ship and deliver the package.

She intended to do just that.

There was no path here, not even game trails, forcing her to dodge back and forth between the trees. Underbrush scraped constantly against her pants as she tried to avoid tripping on raised roots and partially buried rocks, making progress feel hard-earned and slow.

Lousy hiking conditions but pretty good cover.

Not that it would matter if things went badly. She shook out her arms, rolling her neck. Anything to relieve some of this tension. She needed to be limber, focused, confident. Instead, her nerves were so raw, she felt like she could vibrate out of her own skin at any moment.

She paused as they reached the clearing, not stepping into the exposed meadow. And it *was* a meadow. Short grasses and brightly colored wildflowers covered the space, playing counterpoint to the half dozen aliens standing at the opposite end.

Cass couldn't help staring. Most of the species she recognized, even if she couldn't identify them by name. One was a short, aquatic species with wing-like appendages that looked like skin flaps. Its dry gills were fused together, allowing it to breathe air. Another had huge ears and no eyes or nose. It was unnerving, and its green and tan coloring almost blended in behind the rest of the group.

But it was the one at the front that drew her attention most. He made her think of the legends of old, of monsters and creatures of the dark. His pointed ears twitched as his elongated head swiveled back and forth, searching. His sharp, pointed teeth peeked out from between his lips, an ominous portent of this meeting's potential endings.

She swallowed hard. The alien werewolf's hands flexed at his sides and, thank God, he didn't have claws, just hands like any human. He didn't wear clothes, but his thick, green fur covered everything, leaving nothing but his chest and belly exposed where the fur thinned out.

Yep, green fur.

I wonder why it's green?

She shook the curiosity away. *Not the time, Cass.* Goddamn it, *definitely* not the time. She waved to Kou and stepped out of the trees, walking calmly forward. She didn't feel calm, though. It took everything she had to keep her knees from knocking together.

Cass stopped ten feet from them. The leader's dark eyes glared into her, animosity coming off him in waves.

"The crystal," he growled, his long jaw strongly accenting the Usan words.

She reached behind her, working the clasp on the package. Her right hand twitched at her side, brushing over her cargo pocket. Removing the small sack, she tossed it at him, surprised she'd managed it with her non-dominant hand.

Kou was devastated. He couldn't believe she'd given them the package. What's more, he couldn't believe that he'd let her. He watched impotently as the black bag flew through the air and the big, furry Lycaon at the front snatched it up. Kou wanted to dash forward and take it back, damn the consequences, but he didn't, couldn't. He stood frozen, cursing himself for his inaction. But they were outnumbered. It would be suicide. He knew that.

It didn't stop his self-loathing, though.

It didn't prevent him from feeling like a failure once more.

The leader glared at Cass for several moments before turning to the bag and opening it. The bag was wrapped around itself several times, so the moment dragged on as he unwound it. Kou felt like he would explode at any moment as tension continued to build.

He needed a plan. He needed to get the package back. Maybe he could ambush them on the way to their ship? Or follow them and sneak on board?

Kou pulled out of his own thoughts as he sensed sharp motion out of the corner of his eye.

The Lycaon had finally opened the bag. "What is this?" he roared, his voice reaching timbres he'd never heard before in a sentient being.

Kou jerked his head around to stare over at Cass in shock. She didn't give it to them? She *tricked* them? A sick feeling churned in his gut as his body tensed, his instincts flaring to life.

Hacht, we're dead.

"Showtime," Cass whispered.

Then all hell broke loose.

CHAPTER ELEVEN

*C*ass couldn't say what had possessed her. It wasn't money. It wasn't pride. It wasn't even a sense of indignation over being threatened by these assholes. This was just something she had to do, and the plans and preparations had come easily to her, a simple series of steps culminating in this very moment.

Let's do this.

She shoved her hand in her pocket. Her knuckles scraped against the rough material as she gripped the cool, textured weight of a grenade and pulled it out, throwing it as soon as the Diehli were distracted by her fake crystal. Not waiting for a response, she dashed for the trees.

Come on, come on.

The distance seemed impossibly far. How could they ever make it? She kept expecting to get shot in the back at any moment.

Boom!

Dirt and clumps of grass slapped against her back and thighs as she continued to run, her breath sawing in and out. The only sound was the pounding of her heart. She reached the nearest tree, grabbing on to its rough bark and pulling herself behind it. Turning, she let out a sigh of relief at spotting Kou do the same at the tree next to her.

She peeked out as she drew her guns. The enemy was still dazed from the attack and several lay on the ground, not moving. Cass stepped from cover, pulling on the triggers of the automatic pistols. A repetitive jerk pulled at her wrists as gunfire assaulted her ears.

Shouts rang out, and those that could move dashed for cover.

Click, click.

She dashed back behind the tree, leaning against its bark.

"Where the hacht did you get a grenade?"

She turned as he slapped a fresh clip into his gun. She shrugged. "A job." That was one of the benefits of piracy. Sometimes, she stumbled upon things she could *never* hope to buy herself. She had an entire arsenal hidden in the bowels of her ship.

She stepped out of cover after replacing her own clips and opened fire once more. One after the other, they fell until only she and Kou remained.

Cass walked out into the meadow, surveying the battlefield. A large swath of vegetation had been burned away by the grenade, leaving dark brown earth in its place. She felt a momentary thrill of victory, her adrenaline soaring and making her almost giddy.

Then Kou stepped up beside her and a different thrill raced through her. She felt the warmth of his body and was tempted to lean into him, her libido reacting quite positively to the danger they'd just faced. "This won't solve our problems," he said, not even looking at her.

She scowled, the rapid pull back to reality like a rubber band breaking, sudden and painful.

"No, no it won't."

After an inspection of the area that found no one lying in wait, they rushed back to the ship.

"Shouldn't we go after them? Go after their ship?" Kou asked as trees whipped by them.

Cass stopped and looked back at him like he was stupid. Kou bristled.

"And do what, exactly?" She pressed forward, invading his personal space as she pointed in the direction they'd been traveling. "Everything is back on the ship. I brought enough for the threat we anticipated, not taking on an entire crew, let alone a fully functioning ship that probably has offensive capabilities. What we just did bought us time, but we're not prepared for anything else."

"We could be," he said quietly.

She turned back around, stopping with her back facing him. "You're right. We could be. Just not right now. Now, let's get a move on." She broke into a jog before disappearing between some trees up ahead.

Kou felt conflicted as he followed behind her. He *did* feel stupid for suggesting they take on the ship when they didn't have the proper tools. He also felt a blooming respect for Cass. He'd started seeing her in a different light, seeing her as more than just a pirate who only cared about her next score. Who would have ever guessed that she would do the right thing?

Or was he reading too much into her behavior? Was he trying to ascribe virtues to her that she simply didn't have? Was he letting his attraction to her cloud his judgment?

But as much as he wanted to harden himself against her, he had a hard time resisting her. He kept glancing her way, noticing the way she moved, the fit of her clothes, that smile that seemed to always speak of mischief. If she hit on him again, he suspected he would cave, regardless of her motives.

And it wouldn't bother him one bit. They weren't at odds for once. In fact, they were working together toward what he hoped was a common goal. At the very least, she'd resisted giving the package to the Diehli, showing some sort of change of heart, right?

He slowed to a jog as the big, gleaming ship came into view, his eyes smarting at the shine. He slowed further as he stepped onto the ship's ramp.

"Angus, what's our status?" she said as she passed through the door.

"Bots have finished the exterior inspections. I've sent some of them on repairs to the hull but the rest are working on interior systems."

"What can we do?"

"I'll send information to your bracer."

Cass looked down and touched the device on her wrist. "Thanks, Angus." She turned back to him. "Well, what are you waiting for? Come on."

"Aye, aye, Captain," he said, half mimicking the AI.

He followed Cass through the ship like a well-heeled pet. Once in the cargo bay, Cass shifted a panel aside, exposing the guts of the ship, a dark corridor filled with metal and wires. After receiving directions from her, they fell into companionable silence, working side by side in the narrow spaces, receiving intermittent updates from Angus.

Still, the problem of the Diehli's ship bothered him, and he broke the silence. "What are we going to do about the other ship?"

"I don't know," Cass said, pulling back from the task at hand. She looked over at him, her eyes shining in the darkness. "My main concern is getting our ship operational. If we can fly, we can escape them."

"But that didn't work last time, did it?"

"The *Trojan* was already damaged. We tried to enter sub-space but had to exit it almost immediately. We couldn't escape." She paused, taking a deep breath. "Then again, I was surprised, even with the damages, that they were able to follow us at all. Never had that happen before."

"And what if they come to the ship before we can take off? We don't know how large their crew was, and if it were me, I would have left men behind to guard it and prepare for the worst."

She nodded. "Yeah, me too."

They lapsed into silence again as they both resumed their work, keeping their hands busy with the repairs. He had ideas, options, but it would entirely depend on what Cass had on her ship.

They fell into a steady rhythm, an intricate dance as they worked. After a while, they practically anticipated what the other might need before they needed it. He smiled as he handed her another tool, and she smiled back, her mouth tipped up more on one side than the other.

They had a harmony in their actions he hadn't experienced in a very long time. It reminded him of his time in the military, of fighting alongside his unit.

His mind soured, though, when it inevitably reminded him of their end, that gruesome day he would never forget.

Cass wiped some sweat from her brow, exhaustion dragging on her as she leaned against one of the upright beams in the maintenance corridor. They'd spent a good, long day working to fix the ship, and bonus, the Diehli hadn't shown their faces again. They'd received a much needed reprieve, and she hoped it would continue.

Little twinges of fear tickled her nerves, though. Every moment spelled another opportunity for this eye of the storm to end. She needed to deal with the Diehli, but her muscles felt like jello, and she just wanted to melt into the floor.

Putting down her tools, she looked over at Kou and smiled. "So, you want to go to bed?"

"Yes." He smiled at her, his expression soft but worn from the day's trials.

Damn pity, too. She didn't have the energy to try to seduce him tonight. "Come on. This way."

Her movements were slow, her feet dragging. She just didn't have the energy to lift them as rubber squeaked against metal. At her door, she paused, her arm feeling too heavy to lift. When she pushed the door open, it met resistance and her brain fritzed out, unable to comprehend why in her exhaustion.

"What the hacht happened in here?" Kou said over her shoulder.

She shrugged, her heavy-lidded eyes skipping over the sea of clothing coating the floor. "Just try not to fall." She shuffled forward, her feet trailblazing a path through the mess. At her destination, she fell face first onto the bedding. It seemed too much effort to get her legs up, too.

Then, big warm hands wrapped around her waist, and she could just cry because she didn't have the energy to do anything about it. His touch was gentle as he settled her in bed, wrapping the warm comforter around her.

By the time he slipped in beside her, his body heat settling deep into her bones, her eyes were already closed. She fell asleep with his arm wrapped around her.

Cass woke up the next morning wrapped in Kou's arms, his left leg heavy on hers. Looking down, she marveled, seeing parts of him she'd never seen before, not even when he was in medical. He'd broken his right leg, so she never had to see his left, mechanical arm. She touched her fingers lightly over it, wondering how far it went. Was he sensitive? Could he feel anything with it?

"Mmm." Kou woke up sluggishly, rubbing his right cheek against her neck as sleep relinquished its hold.

"Morning, Chad Sexington," she said, a smile on her lips.

"Told you," he mumbled into her skin. "That's not my name."

"But you are sexy."

He froze, pulling away. "No, I'm not."

Cass shifted in his hold. It took effort, too much effort on the soft mattress since they were practically fused together, but she faced him, looking up at his serious face. "Kou." She reached up, touching the left side of his face, the metal side.

He pulled away further, trying to escape her reach, her touch.

"Kou!" She smacked his chest, surprised when she hit metal instead of skin. She was reminded of her earlier curiosity. "How far does this go?"

"It doesn't matter." He tried to escape her, shuffling away across the bed.

"Kou, no!" She sat up, straddling him and holding his back flat to the bed with both hands. He could probably just shove her right off him, but he didn't. "What's wrong? Just talk to me."

He looked away, burying his left cheek against the bedding. "It's nothing."

"Bullshit." She glared at him, but he wasn't looking at her, instead staring off into the distance.

"Huh?" He turned to her, confused, before realizing what he'd done and resuming his positioning.

"Just talk to me, Kou. What's bothering you? Why did you pull away?" She had to admit this was the first time she'd ever straddled a guy without his little helper coming out to play.

But he wouldn't say anything, staying still and tense beneath her, leaving her to try to puzzle it out on her own. Then it struck her. He pulled away each time she touched the metal parts. She looked down beneath and behind her. It covered half his body. What happened to him?

Her gaze softened, and she reached out with her left hand, running the backs of her fingers over his right cheek, testing.

He didn't pull away, didn't move, so she kept doing it. A small smile crept over her face. She liked the soft fuzz he had there, not coarse like a human man's beard, but silky like a Yorkie's coat. Pity he'd lost so much of it from whatever had happened to him, but that didn't matter. He was a live. He was here.

She trailed her fingers over his jaw, down his throat, careful not to touch the metal. Everyone had body image issues. This was apparently his. That was okay. She could work with that. He swallowed under her fingertips, the muscles bobbing back and forth.

Then she moved on to his shoulder. He didn't have a collarbone like humans did, thick muscle sitting there instead, jumping under her touch. She ran her hand over his shoulder and down his arm. They felt human. The hard, round structure of the shoulder, muscle roping over long bones. Though, she frowned, as she slowed down, paying more attention, she realized the muscles weren't in the same places. "Hm."

She dropped her touch to his fingers, slipping hers between them and lifting his hand up. Unlike her thin, see-through nails, his were black, thick, and pointed like claws. She poked one with a fingertip, surprised when a drop of blood welled at the point of contact. She smirked up at him. "Well, aren't you a deadly beast?"

He was looking at her now, wary but focused.

Cass looked away, focusing on his body. That was what she'd wanted anyway, right? She quickly ghosted her fingers up his arm, the muscles twitching under her, before moving on to his chest. Like his arms, his chest, at least the right side, was similar to a human's. She could feel a rib cage under the skin and muscle that traveled down half his torso, but again, the muscles were shaped differently. He had abs and pecs, but other muscles roped around them, making her wonder about their purpose.

One ran crossways to his armpit, a wide band of muscle that covered most of his flank. The muscle flexed, pulling his pecs and abs taut as she ran her fingers over it.

"Don't," he said, his voice tense.

She looked up, her lips stretching into a smile. His face was tight, eyes closed, and he'd started pushing his neck and chest out. She rubbed her hand up and down his chest and belly. "What's wrong, Kou? What do you need?"

He groaned, but didn't say anything, so she ignored the comment. But she'd reached as far as she could from her position straddling his hips. She scooted backward, finding another area where he and humans differed.

"Well, isn't this interesting?" He'd come to bed unclothed, she realized, but seeing as he was as smooth as a Ken doll down there, maybe his people didn't care about nudity. Didn't bother her. It wouldn't be the first time. She ran a hand over his lower abdomen, her finger tracing an almost invisible slit. "An everter, huh?"

He jerked as she ran a finger over that spot, watching the passion flood his face. She could feel his member shifting under that slit, wanting to come out to play. She leaned forward, still rubbing her hand over that spot, and whispered into his ear, "Tell me what to do."

He groaned, his hips bucking upward. Then his tip touched her palm, the silky spot growing until her palm surrounded his length.

"Good boy," she said, pulling at his ear. She leaned back, looking down at what she'd brought about. She smirked. "*Big boy.*" She ran her fist up and down his length, his hips twitching upward as another groan slipped from his lips. He was hot and hard, his smooth skin there in contrast to the silky fur teasing her palms.

Damn, she was still dressed. She looked down at herself. Hell, she was even still wearing the bulletproof jacket she'd donned as protection for their meeting with the Diehli.

She tapped her lip, running her finger back and forth over the soft tissue. "Seems I'm a bit behind. I better catch up." She unzipped the jacket slowly, taunting him, then threw it across the room. The floor was so covered, it didn't even make a noise. Then she ran her hand over her belly, shifting her shirt up to expose the skin there. His gaze dropped down, and she smiled, working the shirt up so it gave teasing glimpses of her bra beneath.

When he growled at her, she laughed, grabbing the shirt by its hem and lifting it over her head, forgetting about it the minute it left her grip. She licked her finger, trailing it down the center of her body. Again, his gaze followed the motion until she stopped at the button of her pants.

She smirked, flicking at the button but not doing anything about releasing it until he barked her name, "Cass."

Cass laughed, working to get her pants off, but tsked when her position kept her from getting the material beyond her hips. "This won't do." She leaned forward, running a teasing touch over his furred skin. "I'll be right back."

Cass slipped off the bed, shucking the pants and boots quickly then, giving him a considering look, she decided to lose the panties and bra, too. She wouldn't be needing them. Advancing like a wild cat, she slinked forward, straddling him once more. This time, the fur tickled the insides of her thighs. She wiggled in place, enjoying the feeling.

Kou's arms flew out, latching onto her hips to hold her in place. She held her breath. That was the first time he'd initiated something since this foreplay began. She gazed down into his eyes, wanting to be sure. Fire stared back, and she smiled.

Finally.

She knelt up, wrapping her fingers around him, teasing his length against her own swollen skin. She shuddered, twitching to get on with it, but this was half the fun, wasn't it? What fun would it be if you jumped straight for dessert every time?

Well, maybe that *would* be fun, but you'd probably end up with an upset stomach.

And she had other things in mind. She leaned forward, whispering into his ear once more. "Do you want this?" She caught movement in her periphery, but she wasn't willing to settle for that. "You'll have to say it."

"I want you."

She smiled against his cheek. "That's all you had to say." She lined them up and pressed down, her breath shuddering out as her body swallowed his. It felt damn good, her insides already quivering. She rested her hands on his chest, one on fur, one on metal, and began that age-old dance. Rising and falling, she took it slow, watching his face, his every expression.

He bit his lip, his hands fisting into the bedding as a groan slipped out. His hips jerked up, the slapping sound it made driving her onward. "Touch me," she said, resisting the urge to touch herself. It wouldn't be the same.

His big hands slid up to her waist, fingers exploring feather-light against her sensitive skin.

She tilted her head back as she rocked. "More, don't stop."

His hands continued up, running hesitantly up the slopes of her breasts, goose bumps chasing after his touch. Then his fingers finally teased over the tips, sending an arrow of sensation straight through her.

"Yes." She moaned, grinding against him harder.

His hips bucked once more and his hands held tighter, less exploratory and more possessive. Then he pinched as she came, a scream ripping from her lungs. She collapsed against him. Her arms reached up, hands curling into his short hair. She pulled his head down, running her lips teasingly over his.

He growled, nipping and pulling at her bottom lip before flipping them over. "Now, it's *my* turn." He lifted up off her, a wicked grin on his face that spoke of good things, before pulling back and slamming his hips forward.

She gasped, her limbs wrapping around him to hold on tight. His tail teased her toes as it twitched back and forth.

Then he didn't stop. Cass's mind went blank, her body awash in sensation as he went to town, riding her like a fucking bronco. Little squeaks she'd never heard before slipped from her lips, unable to take a deep enough breath even to moan. Her entire body was on fire. Then she came again, her breath wheezing out of her.

Kou growled, nipping at her lip again, but he didn't stop, instead shifting his grip and lifting her butt off the blankets. With better leverage, his pace increased.

He's gonna kill me.

The single thought drifted through her head, half formed, half crazed. Her entire body seemed pulled taut. She released his hair, pulling at her own, needing something to ground her.

Then he roared as he came, inadvertently grinding against her clit, knocking her into the stratosphere yet again. She panted as he collapsed on top of her. Sweat cooled all over her body, her skin sticking to his fur where they made contact.

He rolled over, but she didn't want to release him, curling into his side instead with an arm and leg wrapped over him.

Damn, but that was the best sex she'd ever had.

***

Kou lay on his back, his mind full to bursting with Cass. She was a revelation. The way she'd been gentle, careful to avoid his issues while trying to bring him out of his own head. It seemed every time he discovered something new about her, he realized he'd underestimated her. Would he ever feel like he'd gained her measure?

His arm curled around her back as her breaths coasted over his chest, tickling the hairs there. And he realized it wasn't just his mind that was full of Cass. His heart was, too. Though he didn't know if he loved her, he was definitely enamored with her. He wanted to see where this would go. He wanted a relationship with her.

Thinking of her tender touches and words, he thought she just might, too.

CHAPTER TWELVE

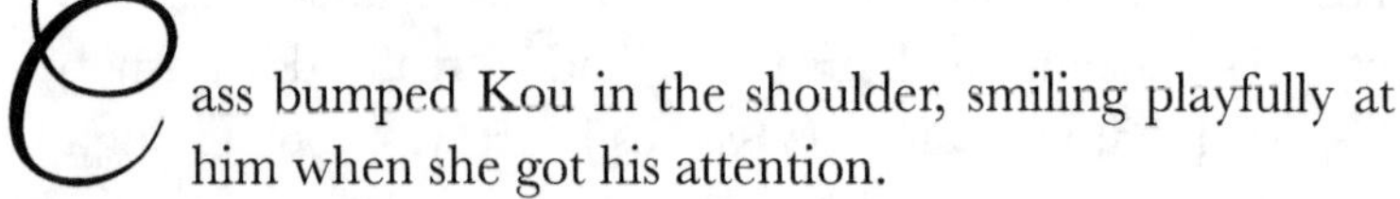

ass bumped Kou in the shoulder, smiling playfully at him when she got his attention.

He smiled back, leaning in to brush a kiss over her lips.

Jess gagged in the background.

Cass laughed as they pulled apart. She really liked working side by side with Kou. He worked hard without complaint, unlike her little sister, and it was always nice having a bit of eye candy in close proximity.

And knowing what he was capable of in the bedroom made the next day one long foreplay session. Every look, every glancing touch, had her thinking about dropping her tools and dragging him back to her room. Or the nearest closet. She didn't much care which. She bet he would be just as good standing up as lying down.

But in spite of her distraction, they made progress on the repairs, and she managed not to think about the still looming threat too often. Oh, certainly, the Diehli would pop into her head from time to time, but then she would glance over at

Kou, he would give her a look, and her blood would turn to steam.

Enemy forgotten.

Of course, it also helped that Angus's bots had made significant progress while they were otherwise engaged.

"Try it now, Angus," she said as she stepped away from the panel she'd been working on.

A hum charged the air as power ran through the circuits. She waited, holding her breath, but nothing sparked, nothing exploded. She let out a sigh of relief. "Okay, what next, Angus?"

"My bots are currently working on the engine repairs. Next on the list is getting water filtration back online."

"Gotcha," she said, saluting with the screwdriver in her hand. "Lead the way."

"Aye, Captain."

Kou smiled as he leaned against the wall of the maintenance hallway, taking a sip of water while his saucy woman saluted the air. Sweet Atala, he loved her sass. His gaze dropped, falling to the twin orbs lovingly molded by her pants.

And her ass. Her ass was mighty fine, too.

She grabbed her tool bag, and he pushed off. "What's next?" he asked.

"Weren't you listening, hot stuff? Angus wants us fixing water filtration next."

He smirked at her. "So, no more trips to that watering hole?"

Her eyes rounded. "God no!" She smacked him. "You have a nasty sense of humor, Chad Sexington."

He stiffened, his arms crossing over his chest. "That is not my name. Why do you insist on calling me that?"

She shrugged, leaning into him, running a hand up and down his tense arm. "Well…" She licked her lips, the pink flesh glistening in the harsh lighting. "See, I spend a *lot* of time on this ship with nothing but my sister for company. A girl gets lonely." She shrugged. "I like to read to pass the time. And Chad Sexington is the main character in my favorite book series." She ran a finger along his chest. "He's sexy and strong and brave and a total badass. Sound familiar?"

He laughed, wrapping Cass in his arms. Sweet Atala, but she was a delight.

Unfortunately, he was also very aware that they still had the Diehli out there waiting to strike. They needed to get out of here. They needed to get the package to his employers. It would be safe then.

He hoped.

Jessie stood back watching this train wreck happening. She knew her sister. She'd suffered through far too many awkward morning-after encounters with far too many species of aliens. Some of them, she wasn't even sure were male. Cass was like a bee, buzzing from flower to flower, collecting what she wanted and moving on.

Kou, on the other hand, didn't seem the type to hop from bed to bed. His gaze trailed her sister with open admiration in his eyes. And most of the time, it wasn't the hunger her sister usually engendered with the barest of efforts. No, the poor bastard was in deep, and she needed to do something about it.

"Taking a bio break," Cass called, waving her hand in the air as she left the room.

Now was her chance. She walked up to the filtration tower they'd been working on and tapped Kou on the shoulder.

He turned, smiling down at her like an older brother.

Great. Just what I needed.

"Don't get too invested," she said, trying to be gentle.

He frowned at her. "Jess? What are you talking about?"

"My sister, Cass." She shook her head. "Don't get too invested. She's not capable of what you need."

A dark expression crossed his face, his entire body going tense.

Oh, shit. Is he gonna hit me?

She moved back a step, ready to run.

"I do not need advice from a child."

Jessie's face burned and her eyes welled up with tears. She wasn't a child. Why did people keep treating her like one? She was seventeen, for fuck's sake! Her jaw quivered, and her hands fisted at her sides. She sniffed. She didn't have to take this.

Fuck him.

She spun around and stormed off. Let him get his heart broken. They deserved each other.

Cass leaned against a counter in the galley. They were all eating while standing, the small, narrow space not offering any seating. The refrigerator hummed in the background while utensils scraped against plates and bowls. "What's our status?" she said around a mouthful of pasta.

She was eager to get this over with and drag Kou back to her room. It had been a long day, and she had every intention of making it an even longer night. She didn't often go for seconds with someone, but Kou was well worth the encore.

"The synthesizer is currently generating patches for the engines. My bots are installing them as they finish, but there's no guarantee they'll hold. We'll need replacement parts as soon as possible."

Cass nodded, surprised they'd even come up with *that* work-around. The synthesizer in the maintenance room was small, designed for replacing small parts or creating patches. It was meant to get them limping along after minor damage that could leave them stranded. It had never been intended for repairs this extensive.

Hell, they'd never *required* so many repairs before. In fact, this was her first time having to do any real repairs on the ship at all. The ship's material automatically sealed minor damage, and she never intentionally put her ship in danger.

But it looked like they would still need Vicky to finish the repairs and get this beast good as new again. Unfortunately, Vicky was about as dangerous as a bunny rabbit. Cass couldn't in good conscience bring her here when a threat still loomed.

She needed a plan.

"Do we have an ETA on finishing repairs?"

"Finishing repairs or getting the Trojan space-worthy?" Angus asked.

She sighed. "Both?"

"Canna finish repairs without proper equipment. Estimate less than 24 hours to space-worthy."

"Good, then you don't need us." Cass shoveled the last of her food in her mouth and dropped her dishes in the dishwasher before grabbing Kou by his shirt and dragging him out the door. "Come on, handsome. You're coming with me."

CHAPTER THIRTEEN

Cass yawned, stretching her arms above her head as she woke up. "Angus, how are the rest of the repairs?"

"My bots will be completing the last of the engine repairs shortly. We will then be able to run diagnostic scans and test all systems."

"Fantastic." Over the last couple days, an idea had been churning at the back of her mind, when she wasn't screwing Kou's brains out or trying to avoid thinking about the Diehli.

Though she'd not mentioned the threat to Kou once they'd returned to the ship, she'd definitely thought about it. She'd worried the Diehli might retaliate before the ship was repaired, the ship taking even more damage, damage they couldn't recover from. The last couple of days had felt like an enormous gamble, a gamble with their lives.

But she'd been afraid to act. She faked at bravado, but actually acting on that bravado was not something she was comfortable with. She knew there was no guarantee any attack she made on the enemy ship would stop them. While she had plenty of weapons on board, they were mostly stolen, and she had no way of knowing how effective they would be. For that reason, playing her hand before all the pieces were in place seemed like suicide.

And so she'd waited, but the wait was over. It was time to act.

Her hands went to her lap, her fingers worrying over each other. "We need to do something about the other ship."

Kou jerked his head up, looking dazed for a second. "Right, the Diehli." He scratched his chin.

Cass leaned forward. "Here's the idea that's been rolling around in my head." She started numbering bullet points on her fingers. "We have no ship-bound weapons. We have no shields."

"We don't?"

She shook her head. "Not enough power. Anyway, besides the point. No weapons, no shields. But their ship is fully functional and, I presume, manned."

"Unless they sent their entire crew to meet us."

"Of course, but assume the worst-case scenario."

"Sure."

"If we can distract or incapacitate their ship at the perfect time, we can pretty much guarantee escaping."

"But how are we going to do that? You said we have no weapons." He paused, looking at her thoughtfully. "Where did you get the grenade?"

Cass smirked as Kou finally caught on to her idea. "Follow me." She waved him on, walking down the hall to the cargo bay, angling for the rooms on the right side of the space. She walked to the last door on the right, pushing it open to reveal an empty room.

"I don't get it," Kou said, staring over her shoulder. "It's empty."

"Oh, ye of little faith. Just watch." She stepped into the room, the black metal walls feeling confining in the small space, and entered her code in a panel by the door. The holographic displays along the walls shut off, revealing the cabinets a bare millimeter behind.

At first, the only difference was the creases in the walls, but when she pressed the first panel on the right, a click sounded before the cabinet door popped open. Behind it, lights flickered on, revealing a small arsenal.

"Well, hacht," Kou whispered behind her.

"But wait, there's more," she smirked at him, continuing the process as she traveled through the room. Each panel was one to two feet wide and ran from floor to ceiling. Each was filled with guns, grenades, missiles, and bombs. Some of the items she still didn't understand the purpose or function of, though she had Angus analyzing them.

"Hacht, I've seen military bases with fewer weapons."

She turned around and smirked at him, leaning against the edge of a door with her arms crossed. "A girl's gotta keep busy."

"Indeed. With an arsenal this size, we can definitely do some damage." His fingers drummed against the doorframe, thinking. He stepped forward, fingers lightly running over some of the contents of the lockers. "We'll need to take them by surprise in case they still have a large crew left behind."

"That's always my preference."

"But they probably don't have much leadership on board or they would have reacted by now."

"True, or maybe they *have* leadership on board, but the priorities have changed?"

He sighed. "If only. The Diehli don't exactly inspire loyalty, but greed? That, they can easily inspire."

Cass ran a hand over a bomb, admitting to herself that she was in over her head. She wanted to speak, to tell Kou what they would do, but she wasn't sure. Her experience was with programming, compromising computer systems. She understood the software and electrical properties of countless ships, but knowing what to blow up? What was most vulnerable to attack? She had no idea. "What do you suggest we bring?"

He scanned the contents. "Almost everything. Better to be prepared."

She nodded. "Okay, let's load up."

He reached for the first weapon.

———

Kou stepped off Cass's ship, feeling like his old self again. He hadn't felt like this since the military, since before the attack. Twin guns rested in his shoulder harnesses, but that was the least of his weaponry. Cass had given him a backpack, loading it down with explosives. He'd stuffed his pockets with more, anything he thought he might be able to use.

"Lead the way, hot stuff," Cass said behind him.

He turned, shaking his head. "Isn't Angus the one who knows the way? Shouldn't *you* be leading?"

Cass shrugged. "You have military experience, don't you? I don't."

He froze, having forgot she knew. The reminder of his military surface brought his own personal nightmare with it, teasing the edges of his mind. "Fine." He turned around, trying to force a calm he didn't feel. "Just give me direction."

"Sure," she said softly, pointing toward the nose of the ship. "That way."

He nodded, but his mood had soured, and he had a hard time reclaiming that previous feeling. They slipped into the trees, and his mind taunted him, teasing him with images of his unit, the feel of flesh burning away, and the shame of his failure.

Kou tried not to look at her, tried to focus on putting one foot in front of the other. He didn't want to see his shame reflected in her eyes. He didn't want to *know* she saw him as less.

She tapped his shoulder, adjusting his course, and he nodded, continuing silently through the rugged terrain. One advantage to missions was talking was discouraged. An overheard word could get a soldier killed, and he'd learned those lessons well in his years in the service.

As they grew closer, the territory began to change. Detritus had been blown back, and he spotted a few felled trees between the upright trunks, telling him they were heading in the right direction. As they continued forward, something shined bright between the trees, hurting Kou's eyes. He squinted as they approached. A large, sleek ship sat in the clearing, a clearing caused by its bulk. Burn marks marred the ground and trees where the engines had done their damage.

He tensed, his mind running over parameters, looking for a weakness, an opening. Yes, *this* was familiar. He hadn't realized how much he'd missed this feeling. Cass stepped forward, and he threw out an arm, holding her back. He didn't want her in harm's way. Now that he thought about it, he didn't want her here at all. Maybe he should have suggested she stay on the ship? It didn't take two people to set explosive ordinance.

But no, any soldier knew you always needed someone to watch your back. He knew that too, and in spite of his reticence, he knew Cass could take care of herself. Just the way she'd handled that last encounter said that much.

Still, he cared about her, and it positively gutted him to see someone he cared about in the path of danger.

I can't protect her.

I can't protect anyone.

Those ever-present words drifted through his head once more, undermining his confidence when he needed it most.

Cass tapped his shoulder, and he turned.

"There's no one outside," she whispered.

"How do you know?"

She tapped her ear, and he nodded. Could she tell just by listening?

He stepped out of the trees and dashed for the ship, hoping he wouldn't be spotted. While maybe he could trust Cass that no one was outside, that didn't mean no one was watching on cameras. And there were bound to be cameras.

Kou hugged his body up against the slick, black hull, waiting for Cass to follow a moment later. She slinked up beside him, rubbing her arm against his. He gave her signals with his hands, but she just looked confused.

He shook his head. Of course, she didn't know Ateles military hand signals. Why would she? He sprinted ahead, keeping his shoulder to the hull, aiming for the primary engines. Like the rest of the ship, the shiny, black material hurt his eyes, giving him a mild headache as he focused on the mild swells of the engines on the sleek ship.

Stopping at his destination, he slipped off his pack, trusting in Cass to watch his back. He pulled the coarse material apart, a zipping sound piercing the air as the bag spread its jaws. His hands reached in, running over cold metal until they latched onto the item he wanted for the job. He pulled it out.

It didn't look like much. Just a thin, black box with magnetics on one side. He slapped it to the inside of the engine, highly aware of the destructive force staring him in the face as he worked. If they turned the engines on now, he would be toast, but the explosive would be most effective with direct access to the engine's core.

He pressed the box firmly in place, a finger on each corner. After a moment, it blinked once red, then green, then blended into the housing.

Now for the rest…

***

Jessie frowned as she paced the cockpit. She stopped, throwing up her hands. "I can't believe they left me behind. Again!"

Angus was conspicuously silent as she resumed her pacing. Why did they keep treating her like a child? She wasn't a child. God, Kou had even *called* her a child to her face. Why couldn't they see she'd grown up, that she could take care of herself now? She didn't need them coddling her anymore.

"Gah!" She stopped, stomping her foot once for good measure. "Angus, bring up all external cameras on the viewscreen and load a map of the surrounding area, tracking Cass's tracer signal."

"Aye, ma'am."

At least *Angus* got that part right. The screen came to life, and she laced her hands together, wringing them hard as she waited for news. Jessie hated waiting. She hated being left behind. She just ended up worrying over what she didn't know. The unknown would kill her someday.

As she sat down, watching the display, her ire gradually drained. She reminded herself that both Cass and Kou could take care of themselves, that they'd already gone up against this enemy once and come out the victors. Clearly, they were going to try it again… without her.

She scraped her thumbnail against her palm rhythmically. Knowing where Cass was, seeing the continued movement, even when that movement wasn't much, reassured her. Everything would be okay.

But would it? Even when they came back, there was still plenty of drama waiting on the ship. She thought back to that damned conversation where Kou called her a child. She should have stood up to him, made him see reason. He didn't know her sister like she did. He didn't know what he was getting himself into. Cass was many things, but she wasn't a keeper. He was going to get his heart broken, and she didn't know how to stop it.

Jessie really liked him. She blushed, ducking her head even though no one could see. She'd even tried hitting on him, which seemed rather foolish now. He was bound to be a lot older than her and from the start, he'd only had eyes for Cass, even when he seemed to hate her guts. She'd been asking for rejection with that failed attempt.

But damn, was he handsome. She didn't know what it was about him that made her think so. She'd met quite a few of her sister's one-off beaus and most left her feeling queasy. What did her sister see in them? She knew her sister was adventurous, but honestly? Sometimes she questioned her taste.

So what was it about Kou that she found so attractive? Was it his sense of command? His determination? His sense of justice? She'd never thought that would be attractive with how she'd grown up, but he made her want to be a good girl.

Too bad she was a pirate.

Her gaze returned to the viewscreen where Cass's signal had stopped moving. Her gut twisted once more.

Time dragged on as the tracer signal hovered next to the enemy ship, leaving Jessie's breath tight in her chest. She wanted to be there, but more than anything else, she wanted her sister to be here… safe.

"Gah! Angus? How long have they been *out* there?"

"Fifteen minutes. They arrived at the ship two minutes ago." Angus seemed alarmingly sarcastic as he spoke, and Jessie glared up at him.

"There's no way it's only been fifteen minutes." It felt like an eternity since she overheard them discussing strategy as they left the ship with a large bag slung over Kou's shoulders. She'd been too late to stop them, too late to ask to join. By the time she'd reached the door, they'd already passed through the tree line.

"I canna change the properties of time and space," Angus said, his sarcasm even thicker this time.

"Sometimes, I really hate you, Angus."

"I can live with that."

"You're not alive," she pointed out, not able to resist the jab.

"And thus why your feelings have no effect on my lifespan."

Jessie slouched back in her seat with a grumble as she crossed her arms in front of her. The AI could really be a dick sometimes.

Time progressed even slower once she refused to engage with the AI. Eventually, she couldn't take it anymore. "How long has it been *now*?"

"Seventeen minutes."

"Fuck you, you fucking bastard," she yelled, pointing at the speaker.

"Aye, but now Cass's signal is moving away from the enemy ship."

Jessie stilled, staring at the screen, Angus's assholery forgotten. Indeed, Cass's signal *was* moving toward the *Trojan*. Jessie squealed, jumping up from her seat and dashing for the exterior door to wait for them.

"You do realize it will take the better part of fifteen minutes for them to return, right?"

"Fuck you, Angus," she said as she picked up speed.

Cass jogged onto the ship, her boots banging against the ramp. Her muscles had been tense ever since they finished setting those explosives and Kou ordered them back. She'd never used those devices before, didn't know their yield.

Was her ship far enough away? Should they risk taking off? Risk getting shot at?

"Come on," Kou said, resting one big hand on the small of her back. "We can watch from the cockpit."

She frowned, but nodded. She hated this. All her career, she'd avoided situations like this. She planned her heists specifically to eliminate all potential resistance. She didn't want to fight and, thanks to her computer programming skills, she'd never had to.

Until now.

That reality seemed miles away. She was having to dig into wells of strength she didn't even know she had. Sure, she played at being a badass, but she'd never had the opportunity to truly *be* one.

"Angus? Status," she yelled as she jogged down the hall to the cockpit. She stopped at the door, staring at the two seats. Her mind ran in circles for a moment. Shit. Where were they going to put Kou when they took off? Vicky had designed the ships with two-person crews in mind because of her and Jess.

Cass turned back to Kou with an expression of chagrin. What the fuck were they going to do? Ellie had more people on her ship now, but they'd needed to retrofit it for the Special Forces team she now housed.

"Fuck it. Jess, buckle up," she said, dropping into her seat and doing up the harness just in case. She turned in her seat. "Kou, I don't know where to put you. The ship only has the two seats for launch and takeoff."

"I'll survive."

An image of him sprawled on the floor of the airlock jumped into her brain and she shuddered. No, that wouldn't do. "Just, hold on until the explosion. We'll figure something out."

He smiled at her, seemingly unworried.

Then again, she was worried enough for the both of them. She turned in her seat, trying to push it from her mind. On the viewscreen, Jess had a bunch of surveillance cams up.

None of them could see the Diehli ship. "Angus, bring up a heatmap of the surrounding area."

"Aye, Captain."

A map in the lower right corner was replaced with her heatmap. She smiled, spotting the heat from their three bodies in the lower right corner and the heat from their capacitors behind them. Little blips of red indicated other systems running.

Another ship rested in the upper left corner of the map. Fully functioning, the ship glowed a more even red from the various systems keeping the crew comfortable. The rest of the map was shades of blues and greens with little bits of red from local fauna.

Cass flinched when Kou gripped the back of her seat, surprising her. She didn't even hear him move. How did he do that?

She took in a deep breath.

Just relax. You're too tense.

But she hated the waiting. She just wanted to get on with it already. "How long till this fucking thing blows?" She threw up her hands, ready to get up and start pacing.

"Patience," Kou said, transferring a hand to her shoulder. He squeezed, working the tense muscles there.

She tried to lean into his hands and forget about her problems, if only for a few moments, but she'd never been any good at meditation. No matter what she did, her mind always drifted to her problems, then dwelled on them until she couldn't take it anymore.

Cass supposed she was like Ellie in that way. She'd met the woman when she was only fifteen to Cass's twenty. She smiled, remembering how angry and frustrated Ellie had been that day. The high schooler had walked four miles to the park after a kid made fun of her appearance at school. Cass had immediately wanted to take the teenager under her wing.

Boom.

Cass jerked as the percussive noise flooded the space, jarring her out of her memories. She glanced up, most of the heatmap flaring white for a moment before settling down. From the map, she spotted little pockets of heat representing fires that still roared after the initial blaze died down.

"Okay, let's get our asses out of here." She turned to Jess. "The ship is locked down?"

Jess rolled her eyes. "What do you *think* I was doing while you were gone?"

Cass squinted at her little sister, doubting the statement mightily. She'd never known the girl to be proactive. In fact, she often had to ask her to do things multiple times.

Aw, fuck it. She'd clean up the mess later. "Fine." She unbuckled her harness, looking down at the seat, then at Kou. "Get over here, hot stuff."

He scowled at her, pausing before walking around and sitting down. "Now what?"

She sat in his lap and drew the harness over their heads, adjusting the length until it could go over both of them.

His arms went around her. "This isn't going to work, Cass."

She shrugged. "I'll make it work." They didn't really have any other options. It was share or risk Kou getting bounced around the cabin like a pinball.

"You could get hurt. No, I can't let you do this." He grabbed her hips, trying to push her off him so he could get up.

"Knock it off!" she snapped, smacking his hands away. "I'm a lot sturdier than I look."

"Cass, please don't do this."

Cass's heart lurched at the plaintive tone in his voice. She shifted sideways, hands still playing with the adjustments. "It'll be fine, Kou. You're not the only one who heals quick."

He tensed, something in his eyes signaling a warning she should heed, but knew she wouldn't.

When did she ever do the smart thing?

"No!" Kou roared, struggling in earnest now, but it was too late. Cass had already clicked the harness in place. His limbs flailed around and it made her think of riding a bucking bronco, although not in a fun way.

"Angus, launch. Now."

Before Kou lost his ever-loving mind.

CHAPTER FOURTEEN

*J*essie wiggled in her seat as they launched, the force of takeoff restricting her movements. She always loved this part. It was like a rollercoaster ride, although she'd had very few opportunities to ride them. Growing up, they'd never been able to afford it, and she'd spent most of her teenage years in space.

Even so, the day Victoria offered them a ship had been one of the best days of her life. They'd been living with a shifter caravan for a while at that point. She could admit it was a massive improvement over her sister working herself to death and Jessie always being alone, but it also left her feeling like a transient.

Most of the caravan had lived among those people for genera-tions. Some, like their leader, Jackson, had *lived* for genera-tions, though she still couldn't figure out how he managed that one. She supposed it must be a shifter thing, but she'd never gathered the gumption to ask. He was intimidating, even if his wife was a total sweetheart.

Victoria had been the one to direct them to the caravan. By then, she'd been living with Cass and Jessie as an emancipated minor. She was a quiet girl, living in her own inner world, with few people ever managing to drag her out of her own head. Mostly, you just lived within her sphere, occasionally earning her attention. Jessie often thought it was sad. Though she had few friends and almost no social awareness, Victoria often went about her chosen work with a determination Jessie didn't think was all that natural.

"Angus, call Vicky," Cass said beside her as she popped her harness and stood, allowing Kou to escape.

Jessie removed her own harness, jumping up to get behind Cass, impatient to talk to Victoria.

The screen changed, showing a small woman with straight black hair falling to mask her face. She raised a single finger, asking them to wait.

Jessie bounced in place, excited to see her friend but also a little surprised. Victoria always pulled her hair back in a pony-tail at the base of her skull. Why didn't she do that today?

The wait was unbearable, but trying to get Victoria's attention was like waiting for a miracle. It was awesome, but sometimes you wondered if it even existed…

"Whatcha working on?" Cass asked, leaning forward in her chair.

Victoria stiffened on screen. Jessie imagined her scowling at the interruption, but then after another minute, she pushed away from her bench-top and faced the camera. "What?"

Jessie grinned, waving at the display. "Hi, Victoria!"

Victoria's gaze shifted, and she smiled. "Hello, Jessie. Doing well?"

She nodded.

Victoria turned her attention to Cass. "Why the call this time?"

"We're coming to visit. We need your synthesizer."

Victoria sighed. "What did you do to my ship this time?"

Cass pointed at the screen. "I didn't do anything. This was *not* my fault."

Victoria stared her down, incredulous. "Like last time?"

<hr>

Cass grumbled, arms crossed, as they started their slow journey to meet up with Vicky. How could Vicky believe *she'd* caused the damage? It wasn't even her fault *last* time. That was a design flaw. The capacitor overheated and shut down.

Not her fault.

Admittedly, she'd been testing the engine's capacities, seeing how fast she could go, and that *might* have contributed, but still.

Not her fault.

Unfortunately, they weren't running at those speeds now. They didn't have full power, so they were moving slow as fuck. Vicky agreed to meet them midway, but it still felt like crawling.

She turned in her seat, looking up at Kou. "Care to go somewhere a little more private?"

He laughed, shaking his head at her, and she smirked.

"Oh, gross," Jess said, covering her eyes and running from the room.

Cass chuckled. "For all she's almost an adult, sometimes she acts like such a child. It's so easy to forget she's going to be an adult in less than a year." She stood, taking Kou's forearm, running her opposite hand over the silky fur as she shook her head. "And she's so impatient to be seen as an adult." She walked toward her room, dragging Kou along with her.

Charging into the room, she kicked clothes aside, focusing on getting to the bed. She was used to the mess, but Kou wasn't. Something heavy skittered across the floor and he grunted, jerking against her arm before slamming to his knees.

He glared up at her as he rose to his feet. "I'm not going any farther with this room like this," he said, waving his hand at the mess.

She looked around and frowned. It wasn't that bad, was it? She'd certainly had it worse before. One time, she had stuff piled on the bed so she could only sleep on the one side. This wasn't *that* bad. She shrugged, not seeing the problem.

"Cass!"

She jerked to face him, dismayed by his body language. No, she wasn't going to be getting into his pants anytime soon. "Kou..." She softened her voice, carefully making the few steps toward him as he crossed his arms over his chest. She raised her arm up to touch him, but he flinched back, pulling out of reach. "We're seriously going to fight about this?" she asked, shaking her head. She couldn't believe it. What was the big deal?

He leaned forward. "Cass, this room is a safety hazard. I don't know how you can live like this."

She waved a hand at him. "It's... You just don't like it because you're ex-military. They probably made you keep everything tidy and spotless."

"That's not the point. The point is it's a miracle no one's gotten hurt already. I'm not going near that bed until we can walk across this room without tripping."

Cass's gaze followed his arm to the bed, an idea triggering in her mind. "Is that a promise?" She posed provocatively, a smirk on her face. She had no intention of getting this room clean, but she could play along for now.

Just think of it as a really *long foreplay session.*

Oh, she could have fun with this.

<hr>

Cass leaned into Kou, rubbing against his organic arm as they surveyed the newly cleaned room. "Well, that was the last of them." She smiled. God, the last little while had been torture, though she hoped it wasn't just her experiencing it. She'd done her very best to rub or grind herself against him every chance she got. When they weren't close, she made sure to bend in provocative ways, accentuating her ass or exposing cleavage.

Kou wrapped his arms around her, his strength pleasing her. He looked around. "Are you sure?" He glanced down, a cheeky grin on his face. "I wouldn't want to trip and hurt myself."

She looked around, but she hadn't seen this much of the floor since they moved into this ship years ago. Hell, she'd forgotten entirely that she'd added padded floor plates, which had been installed for exercise but suddenly had all new possibilities. She smirked up at Kou and wrapped her arms around his neck. "Don't worry. I'll break your fall."

His smile grew. "You will, will you?"

"Oh, yes. I'd be happy to be under you."

He tipped his head back and laughed. "You're too much, Cass."

"And horny," she said, smacking his shoulder. "Don't forget horny." She dropped her hands and ran one over the front of his pants. "And you promised."

He gripped her chin and kissed her hard on the lips. "That I did." Pulling back slightly, his words breathed over her lips, sending a shiver down her spine.

She ground her hand against his length, determined to get him as revved up as she was.

Damn, but right now, she was so wet she could put out a fucking fire.

She reached down with her other hand and started working open his pants. "I don't think we need these anymore."

"No," he said, running a hand through her hair and putting it behind her ear. "I think we can do without a lot of things right now."

She smirked up at him. "Is that your hint that we should both strip? I'm game."

"If you wish."

She laughed and took a step back. He groaned, but grabbed the hem of his shirt, lifting it over his head. Damn, he was beautiful. Definitely built differently, but still tons of nicely defined muscle and the metal just gave him that little something extra that made her want to lick him all over.

Shaking herself, she got with the program, stripping a little too quickly. Her shirt popped a button in her haste and she laughed, but it didn't slow her down. She jerked at her clothes, desperate to get them off, not even caring anymore about enticing him further. She just needed him *now*.

When she finished, kicking her boots across the room to the sound of twin thuds, she returned her gaze to Kou and frowned. "You're behind, Chad Sexington."

He shook his head, that grin still stretching his face, and crossed the distance between them. "I thought I told you that's not my name."

She pointed down at his pants. "And if you were wearing just a little bit less, I might call you by your name, but you haven't earned it yet." She smirked and latched onto his waistband, tugging on it teasingly. "Better catch up, Chad."

"Aye, Captain," he whispered in her ear. His hands brushed hers as he worked his pants off, his erection jumping up to greet her.

"That's much better." She kissed his cheek, working her way to his lips. When she got there, she hovered, whisper-soft caresses teasing but not satisfying. "Now fuck me."

He laughed, pulling away slightly. "Aye, Captain." He grabbed her around the waist and threw her at the bed.

She squealed, landing on all fours, the soft bed bouncing wildly beneath her. She glared over her shoulder, but stopped when she caught sight of him. He looked like a conquering hero, his rapt gaze on her, devouring her. "What are you waiting for?"

"Not a thing," he said as he stepped forward, his hands finding her hips without hesitation. "Hacht, you're beautiful. And so damn fierce."

"Well, this fierce beauty is going to rip you a new one if you don't get on with it."

"Aye, Captain," he said again right before his fingers started tormenting her, touching her so she couldn't sit still any longer.

She jerked her hips at him, burying her head in the bedding. She moaned, her breath coming in ragged gasps, and he'd only gotten started. "More," she pleaded.

He reached around her, working her from the opposite direction as he pressed against her, seeking entrance, teasing her with that anticipatory pressure.

"Do it, damn it!" She smacked the bed, glaring back over her shoulder at him.

He was smiling, damn it. "All in good time."

"No, now."

"Patience."

She scoffed, wiggling backward in an attempt to get on with it. "I don't know if you've figured this out about me yet, but I am *not* patient."

"No, you're not. And you're stubborn as hell. Good thing I am, too."

She groaned, dropping her face against the soft comforter in frustration. "Please," she moaned. She'd been in anticipation of this all day. She couldn't take much more.

He leaned over her, his weight heating and soothing her, and nipped her earlobe. "Very well." Leaning back, he gripped her hips, his fingers digging into the flesh there, and pushed in.

She gasped, pushing back with him, wanting all of him right *now.* "Yes."

He groaned, his body twitching behind and inside her, and didn't move for a moment that seemed to drag on for eternity.

Please, just move. I need this.

Then, as if answering her prayers, he did. It started with one slow withdrawal and return, then he rapidly picked up speed. Neither of them had any control left and the sounds of their fucking filled the air. Slaps of flesh, groans, moans, calling out names, you name it filtered into her ears as she drove herself closer and closer to bliss.

Her body heated like a fever and sweat slicked her skin. She felt like she would go up in flames at any moment. And yet, the moment dragged on. Kou didn't bother touching her, but she was so primed, it didn't matter. She could feel it, like a word on the tip of her tongue.

Almost there.

Almost there.

Kou's cadence changed from rapid, controlled thrusts to a chaotic rhythm with no rhyme or reason.

"Please," she begged, the word dragged out through clenched teeth.

"Cass," he cried out, his deep space brogue making her insides quiver.

Bizarrely, that did it. She came, her body convulsing around him as he collapsed on top of her. He engulfed her in his arms and cuddled her close.

"Totally worth it," she said with a smile.

Kou stood in the cockpit waiting for docking. On the viewscreen, an image of a ship identical to this one approached.

"Prepare for zero gravity," Angus said over the speakers.

Kou gripped the back of Cass's chair, his fingers digging into the swirls of color. Both Cass and her younger sister were strapped in. A smile crossed his face as he remembered Cass's attempts to waylay him while they cleaned her room. He couldn't believe the amount of clothes on her floor. She had more clothing on her floor than he had to his *name*. What could she possibly do with it all?

An image popped into his head of her buying more because she couldn't find what she was looking for. It was quite plausible.

"Initiating docking."

Kou's smile grew. Yes, Cass did *not* like cleaning. At every opportunity, she would stop to strike a pose, lean against him, or feel him up. She even offered to model for him a couple times when she discovered some garment that looked like little more than pieces of string in among the carnage.

Where did I find the will power?

He didn't know and as his body became weightless, his feet lifting off the ground, he didn't care. Once finished cleaning, they'd moved their activities to the bed, then continued up against her desk, the display wall, and eventually had returned to the bed once more, falling into an exhausted sleep.

She was insatiable. He'd never met a woman as amorous as her. It made him want to step back from the physical side of things so they could just *be* for a while, which had actually worked out really well. Depriving her had practically made her self-combust once they'd come together last night.

"Docking complete."

The artificial gravity pulled down at him once more, dragging his feet to the floor.

Cass snapped off her harness, throwing it over her shoulders as she jumped to her feet. "Okay, let's go."

Jess bounced out of her seat, a huge grin on her face. She practically wiggled with excitement, making him forget yet again what Cass had said about her nearly being an adult now.

Kou ushered them both ahead of him as they left the cockpit. Cass moved with barely a gentle clip of her boots against the floor tiles. Jess, on the other hand, moved like a herd of monstrous beasts.

He slowed as he walked behind them, really taking in the hallway decorations for the first time. That was a failing of his —not stopping to really appreciate his circumstances. They were stunning. The planets popped out against a backdrop of deep blue that reminded him of the depths of space or the darkest nights on his home world, Ateles. He ran his hand over one, a brilliant orange and red planet with rings and a single giant storm churning its surface.

Who had painted it? Where had they gotten the inspiration? He could feel the texture of the paint beneath his fingertips as he ran his hand over the wall. He continued to stare at the changing landscape as he followed the girls to the airlock. Blue planets, both with and without rings, gray rocks, and a single blue and white planet that seemed to hold focus over the rest.

He paused over that one, running his hand over the curve of its edge. The artist had taken their time on this one. It was larger than the rest and far more intricate. Was this their home world? It looked so… bright. He frowned, suspecting he wouldn't like it. But if it was Cass's home, surely she would want to travel there from time to time? Maybe the nights would be tolerable?

He moved on, sparing one final glance to that ominously bright planet. He didn't want to think of a future where he wouldn't fit in. As he looked forward, he sped up. The girls had disappeared around a corner. He needed to catch up. Cass wasn't exactly the patient sort.

"Kou, what the fuck?" her voice rang out, making him grin as he picked up his pace.

He jogged into the cargo bay, his steps ringing through the large space. "Coming." His breaths came easily as he slowed to a stop at their side by the airlock.

Cass frowned at him. "What was keeping you?"

He shrugged. "Just taking in the scenery."

She rolled her eyes. "What scenery? It's a ship."

He pointed behind him. "The walls."

"Oh, right. Jess painted them."

He looked at Jess with newfound respect. She painted that? She was just a child. Well, a child on the cusp of womanhood. Still, that she was capable of creating such beauty at any age was an accomplishment beyond words. His people weren't known for their art, but they respected it greatly. Few Ateles showed an aptitude for it, and they tended to be rewarded handsomely for their efforts.

"You are quite gifted," he said, nodding to her in respect.

She blushed, ducking her head so her hair masked her face.

He smiled, enjoying the view as he watched her take the compliment. She was so sweet. She reached over, hiding behind the waterfall of hair, and opened the airlock. Cass stepped through without preamble, but this time Jess didn't follow immediately behind her. Kou watched her for a moment more before stepping through, giving her the privacy to compose herself.

He hesitated when they stepped onto the other ship, faced with a wall of metal. "What?" No one greeting them, not even the woman from the comm.

Cass smacked him on the shoulder. "Relax." She shrugged. "This is just Vicky for ya'."

He stared at her quizzically, wondering what she meant. They turned to the right, walking around what he realized was a massive machine. Around its edge, they stepped into an expansive laboratory. He was taken aback for a moment until he recognized the same basic structure of Cass's space. The walls were the same, though where large pieces of equipment stood here, Cass had subdivided rooms. Where Cass had gear walls, Vicky had lab benches. That was where she sat now, face inches from a computer screen.

As they approached a woman who looked about as young as Jess, she still didn't flinch or move to acknowledge them.

Cass leaned over the woman's shoulder. "You never did answer me when I asked about your work."

"Docking disrupted my work. I had to lock everything down."

Kou looked around, but couldn't see where she'd been disturbed. She was completely focused, even after they'd arrived. This was a friend of Cass's? What could they possibly have in common? How could they have ever met?

"Come on," Cass said, waving her hands in front of Vicky's screen. "Snap out of it for a few seconds and visit with us."

Vicky sighed, rotating her seat around. She stared up at Cass with a put-upon expression. "You're not visiting. You said there was damage to your ship." She pointed at the largest machine behind them. "You can use the synthesizer without interrupting me."

Cass scoffed. "Honestly, why would we come all this way and *not* visit for a spell?" She pulled at Vicky's arm. "Come on, you spend far too much time alone."

"I like it that way," Vicky grumbled under her breath as Cass dragged her off her stool.

"I heard that," Cass said back, but in spite of the tone, there was a grin on her face. She clearly liked mothering the younger woman.

A gentle smile stayed on Kou's face as he watched them interact. Cass would make a great mother someday, not that the two of them could ever have children. His smile faltered. They weren't in a position to think about a long term relationship, let alone kids. He liked her, wanted to explore what they had, but maybe he should take this little reminder to heart. After all, this wasn't the only challenge they would face if they pursued a relationship…

Victoria was annoyed with Cass as she dragged her away from her work. She yanked her arm out of reach and glared, her skin crawling at the contact. Which was when she finally noticed the alien male in their presence. She jumped, staring at him for a moment. He looked familiar, his dark fur with gray markings nagging at her memories, but she couldn't say why. She didn't interact with many, and she was sure she'd never interacted with him.

"This is Kou."

Victoria turned back to Cass, her frustration melting away a little at the hesitance in Cass's stance.

"I kind of stole from him."

Victoria barked a laugh, holding her stomach as she hunched over. She glanced sideways at Cass. "Does he hold it against you?"

She shrugged. "He doesn't seem to anymore."

"Anymore" was probably the operative word. "Where's Jessie?" she said, looking around her laboratory, but the usually ebullient teenager was not within sight.

"She was dragging behind," the alien giant said.

As he took a step forward, she realized for the first time just how big he was in comparison to her own small frame. *Oh boy.* She reached out a hand. "Victoria." Her hand shook a little as his own coarse palm touched hers.

"Kou, Security Specialist."

She tilted her head at him, taking in the cybernetics and bulk. He wore weapons and held himself like some of the military she'd met in the past—ready for anything. And like every guy she'd ever encountered, he seemed to gravitate toward Cass, his gaze and senses zeroing in on her.

Victoria sighed, feeling even more like a misfit than usual. Sometimes, she wondered why she was even friends with Cass. Cass was a good ten years older than her and acted like a mother hen to their entire group. She often felt like less in her presence, but always welcomed her back, like a barely tolerated family member.

"Come on." She waved them toward the hallway. "I'll make us some tea."

Why *did* their relationship work? What kept them together? Her quick mind automatically wanted to analyze them, pull apart the details, and fit the puzzle pieces together. Victoria had tried countless times before, but never succeeded. She could develop new hardware, design ships, work out new technologies, but this was beyond her. She just couldn't understand the social stuff.

Victoria stepped into the galley, absently tapping the display beside the glassed-in robot, and selected four cups of tea. The machine came to life, a robot modeled after a twenty-first century prototype that never took off. Its arms whirred, collecting mugs and tea bags, boiling water. She leaned against a counter in the corner as Cass and Kou filed in, making the space claustrophobically small.

Her natural curiosity eating at her, she wanted to ask Kou about himself, but her tongue remained glued inside her mouth. It was a common failing with her and a contributing factor in her decision to move onto her ship full-time. People tended to take advantage of quiet people, talking over them, taking their silence as agreement, trying to push and manipulate them.

How many times had her parents done so? How many times did they take on grants and contracts with companies and the military before she could emancipate herself at sixteen? She shuddered. Reaching for the finished tea, she took comfort in the warmth the ceramic material radiated.

I'm here, she reminded herself. *No one can take advantage of me ever again. I control who has access to me.*

The affirmations calmed her down, returning her composure. She took another sip of her tea. It was dark and fathomless, like the depths of space. She loved tea and often had empty or half-filled cups lying around her work areas. And she collected cups, choosing designs that made her smile.

With the tea to fortify her, she opened her mouth, hoping words would spill out. "So, what have you been up to, Cass?"

Cass rolled her eyes, her head falling backward. "Ugh, don't ask me that! You don't want to know."

Victoria smiled into her tea cup, amused by the melodramatics. "I asked, didn't I?"

Cass nodded. "Yeah, ya' did. Had a job go wrong. Ended up crashing on some godforsaken planet."

Victoria stiffened, anger rising in her. "You crashed my ship!" Her tea sloshed over the side of her cup, the warm liquid quickly cooling on her skin.

"It wasn't my fault," Cass said, throwing her arms out. "We were attacked."

She narrowed her eyes at her oldest friend. She'd never approved of piracy, but she couldn't control the woman. No one could. "You probably deserved it."

Cass scoffed. "For once, I actually didn't. *They* were in the wrong."

Victoria glanced at Kou.

"It's true," he said, his body language relaxed. "While she did steal something from the ship I'm employed on, the ship that attacked her did so in order to steal the very same item."

Victoria's eyes widened slightly. *How preposterous.* "You're trying to claim that a pirate attacked another pirate. Kind of farfetched."

"Yet 100% accurate," Cass said, trying to pull off an innocent mien.

Victoria smiled, taking another sip of tea. Cass could never pull off innocent. She was too bold, too sexy, too daring. Everything Victoria was not. "So, the ship is damaged?"

"We did what we could. Lot of patch jobs."

Victoria flinched. She hated patch jobs. She liked things orderly and pristine. Patch jobs just made her think of ragged clothes with mismatched patches to cover the holes. "Why didn't you call me?" she cried out, hurt and upset that Cass hadn't reached out to her. That ship was her baby!

Cass shook her head. "It was too dangerous. The other ship followed us there, so we had to handle them before we could call on you."

She pouted. "Well, you could have called me there instead of coming here with a barely functioning ship."

"Hey! I didn't say it was barely functioning!"

Victoria stared her down.

"Okay, so it's not functioning at max capacity," Cass hedged.

Victoria shook her head, her black hair flopping from side to side, sticking against her damp lips, reminding her she'd never tied it back today. She put her cup on the counter behind her and dug in her pockets, searching for something to pull it back with. Finding a scrunchie shoved in the bottom of her right pocket, she quickly wrapped it around her hair, almost sighing in relief.

"Why don't I set you guys up on the synthesizer? That way, you can get back to your lives."

She looked over at Kou. He seemed laid back and content, but he also looked military. They were prone to keeping a calm veneer. And Cass was the least patient person she'd ever met. She couldn't imagine either of them *wanted* to be here.

Anymore than I *want them here.*

But that was beside the point. Cass was family, and family made demands on you. That was just a fact of life. She might not want them here, might grumble and get frustrated when Cass would demand she keep in touch, but there was nothing she could do about it. "Come on," she said, waving them forward. "Let's get you back on your way."

For *all* our sanities.

CHAPTER FIFTEEN

Kou halted on the way out of the ship as Victoria pulled him aside. He looked down at the diminutive woman curiously, wondering what she could need from him. He saw little more than her long black hair pulled back in a queue at her neck. "Yes?"

She looked up at him, revealing limpid brown eyes. "If you want, I can take you home." She glanced down again, shrugging. "Or your destination."

He was surprised, surprised that she'd pulled him aside and even more surprised that she'd offered to harbor him on her ship any longer than absolutely necessary. His experience with her so far had made him feel she wanted nothing more than to be alone again. She'd barely glanced his way the entire time they'd used the mammoth synthesizer to create their new parts.

"Why?" He had no intention of accepting, but wondered about her motivations. She clearly wanted to be alone, so why offer?

She shook her head. "Because you don't have a way out. You're on Cass's ship and by the nature of space, there's no getting off the ride until she lets you."

He frowned. "You think your friend would hold me against my will?" That wasn't the impression he'd formed of Cass, but he hadn't known her long. She was stubborn and rebellious, so he supposed it was possible, but he just didn't believe it. Not yet.

Her head jerked up, eyes wide. "Oh, no. Absolutely not!" She waved her hands in front of her frantically. "Cass is a good person, wouldn't harm a soul. Though," she looked away, "don't tell her that. It would probably piss her off."

He laughed, the heartfelt sound echoing off the walls.

Victoria looked up at him, smiling at his mirth. "To answer your question, though, just because she wouldn't hold you against your will doesn't mean there will be practical opportunities to let you go your own way. I'm offering you that."

He ducked his head down, looking her in the eyes solemnly. "Thank you. Your concern is appreciated, but I'm where I want to be, where I need to be."

Vicky nodded, turning to walk away, but the conversation nagged at him, haunting whispers taunting his psyche.

No, Cass would never hold him against his will. She might drag her feet about letting him go, but she would do it. Even so, his smile dropped increment by increment.

Isn't there somewhere you should be?

Aren't there people who need you?

The haunting whispers dragged reality back to his mind bit by bit, reminding him that he still had a crew out there in danger.

Were they okay? Were they alive? Why had he not thought of them?

Now that he had, he couldn't get them out of his head. Images of his fellow crew-members lying on the floor unconscious arose unbidden in his mind, tormenting him with his passivity. Why hadn't he demanded they go back? Why hadn't he even asked? He'd never once asked Cass about them.

What was wrong with him?

Cass felt great as she stepped back into the familiar space of her ship's cargo bay. Having her ship fixed and good as new again took a load off her shoulders. She sighed, her body filled with energy, ready to move, ready to *do* something. Hell, she would love to *do* Kou, but as she turned to face him, intending to seduce him, most of the weight returned.

The rock, stupid.

There was still the Diehli, still that rock, still the threat. And as long as they had it, that wouldn't end. It was burning a hole in her hold and she wanted it gone.

"Kou, what was your team going to do with the rock?"

"Huh?" he looked up, distracted, like most of his mind was elsewhere.

"The package I stole? What were you going to do with it?"

He looked around, his gaze not lighting on anything for long. "Oh, right. We were hired to find it and deliver it to the company. They would handle the rest."

Cass frowned. "Well, how do you know they weren't just as bad as the Diehli?"

He didn't respond right away.

"Kou?"

"Hm?" He glanced at her again.

What was wrong? What had him so distracted? "Kou, what is it?" She leaned forward, touching a hand to his arm. "I would think you would want to be an active participant in this conversation but your head's somewhere else."

He sagged and rubbed the organic side of his face. "Sorry. I keep seeing my crew unconscious on the floor."

Cass jerked guiltily. *Shit. I forgot about them.* She opened her mouth to speak, but what could she say? He should hate her for what she did, so why didn't he? She racked her brain, trying to remember if she'd told him they would be fine, that the atmospherics would return to normal without issue.

Her stomach twisted as she started questioning herself.

Was his crew okay? Sure, the ship was programmed to put everything back to normal once they left, but what about the Diehli? Did they race behind the *Trojan* or did they assume the package was still on Kou's ship?

Bile rose in her throat, burning a path upward as that terrible possibility became a stomping beast in her mind. It was possible she'd made the worst mistake of her career. She'd left them completely vulnerable, unable to react to an outside threat.

She'd always considered it unlikely that another nefarious group could stumble on one of her targets before the systems came back online, but the Diehli had been right on their heels. If they'd targeted Kou's ship, the crew could have done nothing to stop them.

Cass bent over at the waist, breathing heavily as panic consumed her, the scenario too horrifying to accept.

Oh God, what have I done?

"Let's go check on them," Cass had said. The words rung in his head, just as surprising hours later as they were when she'd spoken them.

Kou was both excited and terrified of what they'd find. He wanted them to be okay. He wanted them safe, but then what? Every outcome running through his head left something to be desired. If they were okay, he had no reason to stay with Cass. Once delivered to his crew, would she just walk away from him? Would she wash her hands of him? He shuddered at the thought, his heart aching.

But if they were dead? What then? That was just as bad. What if the Diehli had stopped to search the ship, killing off whatever crew-members they could find? What if they just blew the ship up, not even bothering to search it?

"Kou," Cass whispered, her hand running softly over his shoulder. "Come to bed."

He followed robotically, his feet following without conscious command. Cass removed his clothes, but for once, ardor didn't heat her eyes. Instead, they held compassion and maybe even guilt, though he suspected he was imagining that one.

She pushed his shirt off with efficient movements, then continued with his pants. Finally, she simply pulled on his hand, urging him toward the bed.

Cass eased him onto the bed, curling her arms around him as she pulled the soft sheets over them both. Her hands teased his skin, a focal point in his chaotic mind, drawing him out of a never-ending spiral of what-ifs and worst-case scenarios.

Eventually, as her fingers continued to caress gently, his mind quieted enough to drift off to sleep.

"No," Cass said, pointing her finger in Kou's face. They'd arrived at Kou's ship not long ago, and her heart had broke a little at seeing it, but she couldn't bend on this, even for him.

He scowled but didn't back down. "I should go."

"No, you shouldn't. You don't have a space suit, and we don't know what we're walking into." She pointed through the window of the airlock, her gut still churning at the destruction she'd witnessed, all her worst fears seemingly come to life. "You saw the damage on the viewscreen, Kou. There might not be life support on board. We have to be careful."

His scowl deepened, his arms crossing over his chest, but he didn't argue again. She remembered the look on his face when they'd approached his ship. He'd been devastated. Cass couldn't blame him. She'd been pretty horrified herself, and she hadn't known or really seen anyone on board. They'd left the ship in pristine condition. They always did.

Well, they left it in the same condition as when they boarded, but still…

They should have been safe. His crew should have been safe. And yet, she knew it was her fault. When the unthinkable happened, they couldn't defend themselves. She'd left them unconscious and vulnerable to attack. As she'd sat in the cockpit, staring at the ship with jagged holes in the hull, she'd questioned her chosen path in life for the first time. Had ships from previous jobs fallen to similar fates?

It was a possibility, a possibility she'd never considered before. She'd always convinced herself that the chances of stumbling upon another ship were astronomically low. But then again, they *were* in space so "astronomically" fit perfectly with the scenario.

As Kou's scowl deepened and his stubbornness, which matched her own, raised its ugly head, she pressed a finger to his lips, silencing him before he even got started. "I'll evaluate the situation and bring back a suit you can wear. Angus is going to lock down the *Trojan*. You need to protect my sister. Just in case."

He nodded reluctantly.

She smiled and rubbed his cheek, purposely avoiding the metal side in deference to his issues.

Cass turned around, facing the airlock, helmet under one arm. Through the window, she could see nothing but darkness. Was there a window in their airlock doors? She couldn't remember.

She opened the inner door and walked through. "Angus. Lock down the *Trojan*."

"Aye, Captain."

The door closed behind her, dropping with a thunk that reeked of finality. She stared at it for a moment, feeling a little nervous, like an intrepid explorer about to enter a dangerous tomb. She shook herself. "Don't be stupid. It's just a ship, and the enemy is long gone. All that remain here are ghosts."

God, she hoped there weren't ghosts. She hoped the crew were all out cold, just waiting to wake up, but she was just a little too pragmatic to believe it.

Cass returned to the display and activated the outer door, which opened soundlessly, making her even more nervous. Why wasn't there sound?

Because there's no noise in vacuum.

That nagging voice couldn't resist taunting her, reminding her of that worst-case scenario she dreaded.

Please don't let them be dead. I can't handle that.

But her practical side kept rearing up, poking her with reality. Life was rarely fair and never gave you what you wanted. Probably, everyone was dead, and she was just kidding herself.

But then the look on Kou's face popped into her head, making her hope all over again. She didn't want to fail him. That would gut her right along with him.

As she stepped out of the airlock, she activated the lights on her helmet. There was no light on the ship, seemingly no power whatsoever, and it quickly grew pitch black, too dark for even her shifter eyes to adjust. She rotated her head back and forth, but the ship looked deserted.

Next to her, suits similar to the one she wore were strapped to the wall, each space occupied.

None of the suits were in use. Maybe no one had a chance to use them.

She took a slow breath, trying to calm herself.

Continuing her exploration, she didn't see a soul, but she also didn't see any signs of violence. Everything was quiet and pristine in spite of the devastation on the outside. How could that be? How could a ship undergo so much damage to the hull and look like an ordinary night shift on the inside?

It gave her chills, goose bumps running up and down her arms in spite of the thermal qualities of her suit. She pulled out a gun, feeling better with the hard weight in her hands. She put one foot in front of the other, weirded out by the lack of noise, the lack of anything.

Then she turned a corner, and a body lay in the middle of the hall. She approached cautiously, not really wanting to know what fate the person had met. She aimed her gun down, the black metal shining in her spotlight's cone of light. The person didn't move, and her stomach sank even further, making a valiant effort to reach her toes. She dropped to her knees, feeling the hard floor grind painfully through her suit. Ignoring the discomfort, she reached out to the person, a man wearing a uniform that matched Kou's. She rolled him over. He flopped onto his back, eyes closed, but she didn't see him breathing.

She lifted her bracer, running a mobile diagnostics program. It was kind of crap, not having the hardware to detect a lot of things, but it should be able to tell a dead person from a live one.

The screen popped up a result: *No electrical signal.*

Dead then. She sagged, but then rose resignedly to her feet. It didn't matter. She needed to keep checking. She needed to know how badly she'd fucked up.

Kou stood outside the airlock, pacing across the floor.

"Relax, Kou. She'll be back."

He turned and glared at the child, who stood lounging against the opposite wall. She raised an eyebrow at him, waiting for his reaction.

He didn't want to indulge her, keeping his mouth shut and leaning against the airlock, arms crossed. Two could play that game. He stared her down, waiting for her to flinch.

She laughed, bending over at the waist. "You're a hoot, Kou." She straightened and smiled at him. "Everything will be fine. Cass will make sure of it."

He shook his head. "Your sister isn't all powerful, Jess. She can't *make* things work out."

She smirked. "Try telling *her* that. I swear, she's been mothering me, Vicky, and Ellie for as long as I can remember and God help anyone who messes with any of us." She shrugged. "It's just her way."

He shifted, standing taller. "Aren't you the same one who said I should stay away from her?"

"Yeah, well, I didn't want you to get hurt."

"And why do you assume she would hurt me?"

"Because she goes through guys like Kleenex?"

He frowned. "What's Kleenex?"

Jess scrunched up her face. "Kleenex is… shit. Um… it's this disposable paper product people use to wipe their noses. The phrase came about because when people are sick, they'll constantly run out of them."

Kou froze, hands flexed at his sides. She "goes through guys like Kleenex?" Insecurities surfaced again, choking him. Did he mean nothing to her? He thought back, his body tensing further and further as he failed to remember a single moment where she said how she felt. She could often be sweet and tender, giving him exactly what he needed, but did that mean she cared?

She tended to arrow straight toward the physical in most situations, which didn't bode well for him. But was that just her personality? She was bold and sassy, loud in life, and he loved that about her. Just because she hadn't said anything didn't mean she didn't care. And he'd always believed actions spoke louder than words. But what actions could he use to speak her intentions for her?

"Kou! Get your hot ass over here."

He jerked, Cass's voice yanking him out of his head. He looked over his shoulder at the open airlock, where Cass stood waving a space suit in the air.

"Suit up, hot stuff. Need your help."

He nodded, taking the material from her hands. It wasn't his, but it would fit. As he donned it, he watched Cass, but she gave nothing away. He clicked the helmet in place and nodded. "Ready."

"Let's go. And don't dilly dally." She turned her back on him, stepping into the airlock.

He followed. "I don't know what dilly dally means."

Her helmet sagged backward with a sigh. "Just keep up."

"Aye, Captain," he said with a smirk, copying the AI's favorite phrase and trying to lighten his own mood at the same time.

She turned back, shaking her head. "Smartass."

"Don't know what that means either."

She stepped into his ship's airlock again. "Keep clear of the outer hatch."

He looked around and checked, shifting his shoulder a little farther inside for good measure. The door dropped closed, then the inner door opened.

Cass looked back, a look of sympathy or maybe pity on her face. He wasn't sure. While their faces were similar and he'd managed well so far, her face was still alien, so very different from his own. Even so, there was something sad about her expression. He was certain of that.

What did she find?

"This way," she said, moving fast as she turned down the hallway.

She stepped over someone and he squawked. They lay still on the floor and he stopped, intending to help.

"Don't bother. He's dead." Her voice was cold, and she continued without hesitation.

He looked down as they passed, noting it was one of the researchers hired for the job. He let out a deep breath, trying to regain some composure.

You barely knew him.

Kou returned his gaze to Cass's back as she moved through the hallway with powerful strides. She was on a mission, a mission he couldn't fathom. What had she found? What did she need help with?

She stopped in front of an open door on the way to the bridge. She nodded toward the entry and disappeared within.

He followed inside, stopping when his gaze landed on the same amphibian researcher he'd found gasping for breath when Cass and her sister boarded their ship days ago. Her teal skin had almost no color left, and she wheezed with every breath. How was she breathing?

"This is the only one I found alive, but we need to be quick. Her breathing is labored, and I don't know shit about her species."

He nodded and knelt beside her, ready to lift her into his arms.

"Careful," Cass said, kneeling across from him. "I wasn't sure if she was injured."

He looked down, but didn't see any wounds. But then, he was no more familiar with her species than Cass was. "Should we get a stretcher?"

"I'm afraid it would take too long. I thought about just carrying her myself, but was afraid I'd conk her on the head or something."

Conk? He nodded, carefully stretching his arms beneath her frail form. She was long and lanky, designed to move through water, but it meant she dangled precariously over even his large arms. He glanced over at Cass. Even if she could have lifted the woman, her long limbs would have been dangling dangerously close to walls or tripping her up.

Kou turned and walked sideways through the doorway, trying to keep the past from rearing its ugly head. His feelings of inferiority, his fear of failure, taunted him, reminding him over and over that he was useless. This was the best he could hope for—complete and utter failure that got everyone around him killed. What else could he have expected?

He swallowed hard and tried to focus on the task at hand. "Let's go."

They moved as fast as they dared through the ship. Kou checked constantly to make sure their charge still breathed and that he wasn't slamming her into things. It took mere moments to reach the airlock where Cass did the honors. Now, he realized she had a second reason for wanting his help. She couldn't carry the woman and handle the doors at the same time.

Once the airlock opened, he surged past Cass, heading to medical with laser focus. He didn't even register the intervening distance until he dropped her awkward form on the bed. "Angus?"

"Aye, sir. Performing scan."

He sighed, but already he could see she wasn't wheezing like she'd been when he first spotted her in that small room. Still, she looked sickly, her skin dry and pallid, reminding him of a dead fish.

"Will she be okay?" Cass asked, touching his shoulder from behind.

He shook his head. "I don't know."

CHAPTER SIXTEEN

"*L*et me," Jessie said, nudging Kou aside. "Get some rest."

He looked up, eyes bleary with lack of sleep. His entire form sagged with exhaustion. He nodded and rose slowly to his feet, shuffling out the door.

She watched him leave, feeling sorry for him. He hadn't had the best time of it lately. Jessie had never expected they would find his ship destroyed like that. She shook her head, turning back to watch over their patient. The alien woman was still unconscious, though she looked better. Jessie remembered peeking in on her and thinking she looked white as a sheet, but now her glistening skin made her think of tropical waters.

"Maybe you'll wake up soon," she said to the unconscious woman as she sat in the seat Kou had vacated. "It would be nice to have another person on board. Cass and Kou are kind of involved with each other, so there hasn't really been anyone to talk to for the last few days."

She paused, frowning down at the woman. The room hummed with the active medical equipment as her mind fretted over how her life had changed recently. Before this most recent job, she would have never imagined her sister getting so involved with a man, even in prolonged confinement together. It just wasn't how she saw her sexually liberated sister.

And now, she actually felt kind of bad about warning Kou about Cass's history. It was the truth, but did it actually help him? Did it prevent any heartbreak? Or did she just accelerate that inevitable pain? Maybe it would have been kinder to leave him in ignorance a while longer?

Or maybe I'm wrong about her entirely.

She sighed. "Sometimes, I don't understand people. Why can't they just make sense? Do you ever have that problem?"

She smirked. She was asking an unconscious woman questions. How stupid was that?

Cass let out a sigh of relief when they approached the space station. An image that almost reminded her of a tentacle monster filled the main screen of the cockpit. "This is it?" She turned to Kou, raising an eyebrow in question.

"Yes, this is Inia Station."

She looked out, but while bigger that usual, it was much like any other space station. It stretched out in wings and circles, making Cass wonder how they managed artificial gravity for it. Her ship worked off a central axis that it rotated around, but she couldn't spot one for the station.

"Angus, ring 'em up on the comm."

"Aye, Captain."

The screen changed, a male with mildly lupine features filling it. He had deep, dark eyes with almost no white, pointed ears that twitched at each sound, and a mouth that jutted out just a little. Unlike Kou and Zee, he didn't have fur, but a thick puff of hair haloed his head. "This is Inia Station. State your identity and business."

Kou stepped forward, pressing against the back of Cass's chair. "I'm Security Specialist Kou, and we're here to deliver a package for the Omni-Surge Project."

"One moment, please."

The screen went dark, and they waited.

What was the Omni-Surge Project? It sounded ominous. She turned around, looking up at Kou, but he gave nothing away. Suddenly, the curiosity that she'd kept easily at bay ate away at her. She wanted to know what she had in her hold. What was it worth? Did it do something? She suspected it did, or else why would anyone go to such lengths to retrieve it?

"I don't have a 'Kou' associated with that project."

Cass watched as Kou's body went tense, his face slipping into a more severe, but blank expression. What was he thinking? What was he feeling? Cass suspected there was *something* churning under that calm facade, but she didn't know what. She wanted to reach out to him, soothe him, but didn't think it was the right time. She turned back around, watching the events unfold.

"I was hired by Captain Eev Welgan."

The man looked down, nodded, and looked up again. "Yes, I have that name on the project roster. Where is Captain Welgan?"

"Dead," Kou said, voice deadpan.

The station employee jerked back but otherwise didn't respond, simply jotting down something on a surface offscreen. "I'm sending docking coordinates. You will be met in the docking bay."

Kou nodded. "Please ensure a medical team is present at the dock. We have an injured crew-member on board."

The man nodded, jotting something else down. "It will be done." Then, he reached forward, and the connection died.

Cass looked up at Kou, but he didn't look at her in kind. He stared off into the distance, the same withdrawn man he'd been since they rescued the woman from that ship. She figured it was probably trauma. He'd been through so much. Still, she missed him, wishing he would come back to her. Things had been surprisingly platonic since leaving his ship behind, possibly even more so than before they'd fallen into bed together. And she hadn't thought that was possible.

But he barely looked at her anymore, and she didn't know what to do about it. She'd never tried to romance a man beyond a one-night stand before. She really was out of her depth here. How was she supposed to navigate his moods? They seemed as changeable as the winds.

As she continued to watch, trying to come up with solutions in her head, Kou turned, not even looking her way, and walked out of the room.

What am I going to do?

Jessie beamed at Kou as he entered the cargo bay. "Are we ready?" She wiggled in place, youthful ebullience getting the better of her. "Should I get it?"

He stared at her, looking confused, which was probably more expression than she'd seen on his face in the days it had taken them to reach the station. She tried to hold onto her excitement, but it drained out of her little by little. She'd now kicked herself countless times for warning Kou away from her sister, feeling she'd caused this rift somehow.

Why did I do that? How could I have been so stupid?

She'd thought she was doing the right thing, saving him some heartache, but Cass had been taking Kou's behavior really hard. Jessie would almost say her sister was pining after the man, and she would have never thought her capable of that.

But the two of them had been impossible the last few days, with Kou walking around like a living ghost, and Cass following him around like a lost puppy. She'd never seen her sister so uncertain before. Even when Jessie was just a little kid and their parents had just abandoned them, Cass had always acted like she had it all covered, like nothing was wrong. Jessie knew better, but Cass refused to admit it out loud.

Could her sister finally be falling for someone? It seemed farfetched, like a fantasy or Science Fiction movie. Then again, they *did* live in a spaceship, and that used to be the realm of Science Fiction, so why not?

Cass entered the room, her usual swagger in place, but her gaze immediately searched out Kou, who stared blankly at the airlock. Jessie dragged her focus away, moving over to her sister.

"The patient is secure and Angus should be docking shortly," Cass said.

"Yes, Captain," Jessie said, mockingly saluting her sister, hoping for a smile. Cass could use a smile.

Her sister rolled her eyes. "Smartass."

Close enough. "Should I get the package?"

Cass nodded. "Yeah, go for it. We'll be handing it over shortly."

Jessie nodded and bounced off, stopping in front of the first "room" against the right wall. They weren't locked, and she stepped right in, moving to the inner panel that controlled the camouflage. She entered her personal code, and the compartments were revealed. In a couple steps, she reached the one in the corner, pushed the panel, and it popped open, revealing the glowing blue rock.

Man, it was pretty. She wished they could keep it. She wouldn't mind putting it in her room somewhere, but it had already caused them enough trouble. They didn't need any more.

She grabbed it, feeling the smooth crystal fused to coarse black rock. Of course, it *had* brought them Kou, and that seemed to be a boon for her sister.

If only she could get her shit together.

No guarantees there, though.

She walked from the room, expecting some comment from Kou, but got nothing. He didn't even notice her. She wanted to snipe at him, tell him to snap out of it, but she didn't. She couldn't imagine losing her entire crew. Her entire crew was her sister, and that loss would destroy her.

"Ready!" she said, holding the rock aloft.

"Prepare for loss of artificial gravity," Angus said over the speakers.

Jessie hugged the rock and grabbed onto the doorframe with the other hand. She smiled, looking forward to zero gravity.

She loved the feeling of weightlessness, like swimming only without getting wet.

Too bad they couldn't do it more often.

Time stood still for a moment, like a breath held, as the forces pulling her toward the floor let go, causing her to float. She grinned, wishing she could let go, but she knew it was only temporary. Soon enough, gravity would reassert itself and she would slam to the ground if she wasn't careful.

A few seconds later, the moment ended and someone slammed to the ground off to her left, hopefully feet first. She hugged the crystal to her chest, turning to face her sister and Kou. "Ready?"

"Let's do this," Cass said, leading the way to the airlock's controls.

Jessie was farthest from the door, so in spite of Kou's malaise, he reached it before her. She stared at his back, a wall of gray that continued above her head. His hard muscles stretched the soft fabric of his shirt, making her want to touch. She resisted.

He thinks you're a child.

The reminder hurt, but was necessary. It wouldn't always be this way. Someday, she would be seen for the woman she was. Someday she would step out of her sister's shadow.

As she stepped through the airlock, she knew today would not be that day. Cass boisterously greeted someone in brightly colored, shimmering fabric that Jessie caught peeks of around Cass and Kou's backs. Jesus, it was like trying to see around a wall.

"The patient is in our med bay. Angus, our AI, can guide you there," Cass said.

A series of people in white coats and burdened with gear passed around them, slipping into the ship.

"This way," their guide said in a masculine voice once the medical staff were inside.

Of course, she could be wrong. She wasn't exactly an expert in aliens, and gender was such a weird thing even on Earth.

She looked up and around, but there wasn't much to see. They'd docked in a long hallway lined with many airlock doors. She lost interest quickly, the bounce in her step fading as the distance dragged on.

Jessie had hoped to see something a little more interesting on this trip. So far, this hall was even drabber than *their* ship. At least Cass had given her license to decorate. And they hadn't encountered a single being other than their escort since docking. What was with that? Was that normal?

"Through here," he said.

Jessie didn't pay him much mind, just following and nearly treading on Kou's heels. Then she caught her first glimpse of their guide as Kou turned to the right where an open door waited. The man was short and squat, maybe even considered overweight for his species. He had the same lupine features as the guy on the call earlier, but there was something in his eyes that made Jessie hesitate.

"Hello," she said, drawing up short. In the room, Cass and Kou had their backs turned, not noticing Jessie had stopped.

The man looked down at her chest, at the crystal hugged there. Avarice gleamed in his eyes.

Alarm filled her. Something was *very* wrong here. She just knew it! Her heart pounded in her chest as she hugged the rock tighter and opened her mouth, preparing to warn Cass.

She didn't get the chance. Before air could pass through her vocal cords, he lifted a weapon and fired.

CHAPTER SEVENTEEN

A shot rang out and Cass flinched, then spun around, looking for the shooter. Through the doorway, that damned glowing rock tumbled from her sister's hands and clattered to the floor, distracting her for a moment from the horror playing out.

Jess had her mouth open, her hands twitching at her chest. She didn't move, just stood there as the moment dragged on. Beside her, Kou seemed to have snapped out of his melancholy. Now, a tension and anger vibrated through his frame.

Then time sped up again, and Cass screamed as her sister slumped to the floor. "No!" She rushed forward, but even though the distance between her and the door was small, a hand still came out of nowhere, slamming the door in her face. She banged on it. "Jess!" Her heart pounded in her chest, deafening her, keeping her from thinking.

"Cass. Cass!" Kou yelled as he yanked her from the door.

Her hands hurt from banging on it.

He spun her around. "That's not helping. We need to get through the door."

"Right." She nodded and smiled at the control panel by the exit. Some of the tension left her as she started pulling out tools. "No big deal," she mumbled as she popped off the panel and got to work.

Moments later, the door slid open, and she rushed through, a weapon already in hand. Anger blinded her as the opening exposed Jess's prone, bleeding form. She looked left, then right, and threw the knife in her hand when she caught a glimpse of bright fabric. "Get him," she said to Kou as she dropped to her knees by her sister's side.

"Aye, Captain." He jumped over her kneeled form, and his heavy footfalls serenaded her as her hands reached for the bloody fabric.

"Jess? Jess, talk to me." She pressed down on the wound, wishing she knew more about biology or anatomy or something. "Jess?" But her sister didn't respond and panic choked her. "Help!" she screamed, her voice going hoarse as she screamed it again and again.

Still, blood seeped through her fingers, staining her hands. It just kept coming.

A hand touched her shoulder, and she flinched, ready to fight.

"Easy," Kou said.

But she ignored the comfort he tried to provide. "Did you get him?" she asked, voice hard as granite.

"Yes." He stepped back, his heat no longer crowding her.

"Get help," she said, her voice deceptively calm. Inside, her head and heart felt like a hurricane. Everything was chaos, thoughts and emotions flying about at speeds too fast to be recognized.

"Right," he said, then she was alone.

She stared down at her little sister, daring her to live, daring her to keep breathing.

This can't be happening.

This can't be real.

Why is this happening?

Wasn't I doing the right thing?

Cass sniffed, only then realizing tears poured down her face. She looked up, panting, surprised when her gazed locked onto a hoard of people running down the hall straight at them. Her mind was too wrecked by chaotic emotions to recognize the uniforms, symbols, or gear, but she spotted one of them holding a stretcher and sighed in relief.

They raced up to her sister, pushing Cass aside. Her bloody hands hovered in front of her, wanting, needing, to do something. She lost track of time as they loaded her sister on the stretcher and raced off. Cass ran behind them, focused only on one thing—Jess.

They burst into a room. Voices yelled. Chaos ensued. Cass was pushed back by someone in a uniform. She tried to protest, but Kou held her back, thanking the person.

For one far too brief moment, she reveled in his warmth, his strength. She didn't want to be strong anymore. She didn't want to fight anymore, to struggle for every little thing.

Why did these things always happen?

"Shh," Kou said in her ear, running a soothing hand over her arm. "She'll be fine. Just wait. She'll be fine."

Anger and pain rushed to the surface, pushing back the fear. She shoved out of his arms, facing him with a finger in his face. "You don't *know* that!" She waved her hands around the room. "This is life! This! Loss and pain! Life doesn't give you anything. You have to take what you need or it'll stomp all over you. Do you think the cosmos cares if Jess dies? Fuck no!"

"Cass," he said, arms out placatingly.

"No!" She shoved him back. "I don't need this. I don't need you. I don't need anyone." She shook her head. "You're just a fuck. I don't even know why I bother."

<hr>

Kou froze, his mind reeling, Cass's words ringing through his head.

You're just a fuck.

I don't even know why I bother.

He remembered those conversations with Jess. He remembered her telling him, warning him, but he wouldn't listen. Instead, he'd treated her like a child, ignoring her advice. Why didn't he listen?

He stared at Cass for a moment more, not really seeing anything, then turned on his heels and left, bumping into someone just entering the waiting room. "Sorry," he said, trying to move out of the way.

"Security Specialist Kou?" the man asked.

Kou jerked his head up, surprised to hear his name. "Yes?"

The other man tilted his head to the side, exposing his neck. His dark brown hair waved around his pointed ears. "Inia Surg, owner of Inia Intergalactic."

Kou looked at him funny, not sure how to respond. What was the man doing?

Surg straightened, the bulging tendons relaxing. "I'm sorry about your crew." His eyes held an almost icy intensity that belied his sentiment as he shook his head, muttering under his breath. "Damned Diehli."

"How did you know?"

Surg jerked to attention. "Know what?"

"That the Diehli killed them?"

"Who else would it be?" He looked over Kou's shoulder into the medical suite. "Do you want to take a walk?"

Kou thought of the verbal lashing he'd just received and nodded. "Yes. Yes, I do."

Cass paced the waiting room, which had comfy couches and was filled with soothing fabrics and paints.

It didn't help. She still felt like she was about to climb out of her own skin.

What was taking so long?

What was happening with Jess?

Was she okay?

Would she survive?

Cass pulled at her hair as she turned at the wall, repeating another circuit of the room. Why couldn't anything ever go right in their lives? Hadn't they been through enough? Hadn't life put them through enough? It wasn't fair!

Life isn't fair.

She stopped, focusing on that ever-present reminder.

Life isn't fair.

It calmed her a little, just enough to stop the pacing, but her thoughts were stuck on Jess, obsessing over her wellbeing. "She's gonna be okay. She has to be."

Someone in a uniform stepped into the room from the inner depths of the medical suite. "Are you the family?"

Cass jerked her head up, registering nothing but the soothing uniform he wore. "Yes."

He looked down at a tablet in his hands. "She's going to be fine. I just have a few questions to help with her care."

Cass nodded, walking up to him. "Anything."

"First, what species is she?"

Cass paused, not sure how to answer. It was a complicated question. Nobody really understood shifters, even after all these decades. Shifters, logically, were resistant to being experimented on, so medical and scientific advancement was slow. "She's a shape-shifter from Earth. Natal form is human, *homo sapiens sapiens.*"

He stared at her like she'd grown a second head, his hand hovering over the tablet.

"What?"

He looked down at the tablet, then composed himself before meeting her gaze once more. "I'm not sure what any of that meant. Earth is..."

"Our planet."

He jotted some information down. "Species?"

"Complicated."

He scribbled that in, too.

"Don't write that down," she said, reaching out a hand.

"What?" His head bobbed up.

She sighed. "We're shape-shifters. We don't have a species name, but it means we're usually a combination of our species characteristics and our current form."

"You'll have to clarify."

She sighed again and sat down on a couch across from him. "We can physically alter our appearance and biology."

"Fascinating," he said, sitting down across from her, gaze rapt. "Continue."

"If you have something I can download to, I can provide details on anatomy and physiology for her current form, which is human. Beyond that, shifters don't have human reparative features. Meaning she needs to eat. Without nutrients, she won't heal from her injuries."

"Why not?"

Cass shrugged. "I don't make the rules. Food fuels shifting. Shifting fuels healing. Everyone knows that."

"But I've never met your kind."

Cass stared off at a wall where a colorful painting took up most of the space. If she'd been in a different mindset, the painting might have soothed her. At the moment, she just felt tired. She shook her head, dropping her face into her hands. "Just make sure she has sufficient nutrients. Everything else will take care of itself."

"How much is sufficient?" He'd returned to focusing on his tablet.

"Too much. Way too much."

He laughed. "She's not full grown, is she?"

A half-hearted smile crossed her face. "Almost. Still practically eats her body weight every day, though."

He laughed. "I have a near-adult myself. It's impossible to keep up with his nutrient needs, and he's impatient to become an adult."

She smiled. "So is she. She gets so upset when I don't see her as one."

"Mine too!" He laughed, the sound jarring her out of the conversation. It was weird, almost like a howling or hooting. "Come," he said as he settled down. "I'll take you to her room."

"Thanks." She followed behind him into a hallway painted a pale blue, then he ushered her into a room where Jess lay in a bed motionless. She stood in the doorway, unnerved by the unnatural stillness. Her sister was never still. She bounced around like she couldn't contain her energy. It felt wrong for her to just lay there like a statue.

But then the doctor walked away, and she stepped inside, sitting in an overstuffed pastel green chair by the bed. She reached out, taking her sister's hand, and her mind finally let go.

Jess is okay.

She's going to be fine.

She looked good. Good color to her skin, breathing easily. It put Cass further and further at ease the longer she sat there, her thoughts finally returning to their more ordered nature.

And then she finally remembered the conversation with Kou. She smacked her hand to her forehead.

I'm so fucking stupid. Why did I say that?

She shook her head, a little shocked at the words that had come out of her mouth. Sure, she was brash and had never even entertained the idea of more than a one-night stand, but she'd never been cruel, and remembering the look on Kou's face, she'd *definitely* been cruel.

"And he's more than a one-night stand." She couldn't deny it. She'd never gone for seconds before, never cared what men thought of her once she left them in her dust.

But she cared, didn't she? Cass wanted to go to Kou now and apologize. But she couldn't leave Jess's side.

And what would she say? She was no better at apologies than she was at relationships.

My pride wouldn't help either.

She snorted. Yeah, she would probably go up to him to apologize and end up insulting him instead. Would probably say something like, "What do you expect? This is me we're talking about."

She shook her head. Yeah, this wasn't going to go so hot.

She'd really fucked up badly.

Kou closed his mouth as he finished filling Surg in on what had happened since they collected the package.

Surg was not what he'd expected. First, he hadn't expected the proprietor of the company to meet him personally, but maybe with the fiascos surrounding this rock, the man had felt he *needed* to step in.

Or maybe he was just that hands on. He'd certainly seemed very practical and approachable since introducing himself at the medical suite.

"Here," Kou said, reaching into the largest pocket in his pants. After dropping Jess's attacker, he'd taken the package back and stored it away for safekeeping. It bulged a little, but remained unseen until his hand displaced the fabric flap on his pocket, revealing a blue glow. "The crew didn't have a chance to do any research on it before everything went to hacht, but I'm sure you have people for that."

Surg nodded, accepting the glowing rock that had caused them so much trouble. He held it in one hand as they continued down the hallway. "I noticed you were having difficulty with your female companion."

Kou bristled, but it wasn't like Cass had been discrete. The proprietor couldn't have helped overhearing. "Yeah, I should have seen it coming. There were all the signs, and her little sister warned me. I guess I was too stubborn to listen." He shrugged it off.

Surg stopped him with a hand on his shoulder. "I wouldn't be so quick to judge her. Don't forget what she's going through."

Kou stared at him, incredulous. Why was this man giving him advice on his love life? It was beyond strange.

Surg laughed and shook his head. "The look on your face is priceless."

Kou scowled.

"Easy, easy." Surg extended his hands placatingly. "I meant no offense." He turned away and continued walking. "Partners are very important to my kind." He didn't turn around to speak to Kou, keeping himself closed off even though his body language was open. "We treasure them, and though selection is often easy, biological even, wooing and keeping them is not." He stopped and turned, staring Kou in the eye. "It takes work, but it's worth it. Don't give up."

Kou was taken aback, stopping dead in the middle of the hall-way, surprised by the change of topic. "You don't understand. I was already told. She's not interested in a relationship."

Surg stared at him, stared *into* him. "You're lying to yourself."

"I am not!" He stormed up to Surg and grabbed his shirt roughly in one fist, but the stark loneliness in the other man's eyes stopped him cold. He let go and stepped back, not able to look the other man in the eye.

Whether Kou believed Surg or not, he didn't have the heart to continue the conversation.

<hr>

With a quiet click of the door closing, he stepped into an empty, unused room. Across from him, a communications console sat against the wall with a single chair in front of it, the only furniture in the room. The console was small, so small he often marveled at how powerful it was. A single device this size, barely larger in height and breadth than his hand, could send messages almost limitless distances across the stars. He shook his head.

Marvelous.

But he wasn't here to marvel over technology. He had a mission, a job to do. And sending this message would get him one step closer to completing it. Soon, his unfortunate stint at Inia Intergalactic would be over, and he could go back to his real life. He thought of his family waiting at home for him, waiting for him to return from this business trip.

Then he thought of the man who was caught just hours before, killed by a member of security, he'd heard. He hadn't really known him except in passing. They'd been assigned the same job together, but the particulars of said job hadn't lent well to personal conversations.

Still, as he stood there, staring at the console, he couldn't help wondering about the man's personal life. Did he have a family? Were there people back home who would miss him, wonder where he was and when he would return home? Would they continue to wonder, never knowing that he'd died on this mission? He shuddered. That would *not* be him. He was finishing this job. He was going home.

He had to.

CHAPTER EIGHTEEN

Jessie woke up in pain, though she couldn't for the life of her figure out where it hurt.

Everywhere. It hurts everywhere.

Jessie opened her eyes to a pale blue ceiling reminding her of a midday sky and frowned. She couldn't be outside. She was laying in a bed wearing some sort of dress. Looking down, she smiled at the brilliant splashes of color on what she assumed was a hospital johnnie.

"Thank God," Cass said, jumping to her feet. "You almost left me there."

Jessie froze, eyes wide, as Cass's wording clicked in her head, solving a puzzle that hadn't made sense until that very moment. Cass was afraid. After their parents abandoned the two of them, nothing scared Cass more. That was why she jumped from guy to guy.

She thought about Kou, who she suspected loved her sister. Her sister might even love him, but she would never admit it or act on it as she was now, would she? The thought of rejection was too terrifying. Jessie could relate, but was that any reason to stop trying? Was that any reason to let fear drive you? She looked up at Cass, seeing the truth written all over her face. The fear was in the driver's seat. "You have to get past this."

"What? Jess?" Cass said, reaching out and cupping Jessie's hand with both of hers.

"Your fear. You have to get past it, or you'll always be alone."

Cass smirked, shaking Jessie's hand. "I'm not alone, stupid. I've got you."

Jessie shook her head. "You won't always."

Cass tensed, her hands gripping tighter on Jessie's. "Don't say that."

Cass's eyes pleaded with her, but she couldn't relent. "You are a good sister, and I would never completely leave or forget you. No matter what distance separates us, we'll always be in touch, okay? But I'm almost an adult now. I don't know what I'm going to do, but someday I might choose to leave your ship. You *would* be alone."

Cass's hands trembled, tears welling in her eyes, but she didn't say anything and didn't let them spill down her cheeks.

"I think Kou loves you. I'm positive he wants to stay. But if you don't get your shit together, he's gonna run in the opposite direction. You're gonna drive him away."

"Maybe I already have," Cass said under her breath.

What?

Kou arrived in a laboratory on Surg's heels. He stopped, taking in the clean, unused space. Before his current job, he probably wouldn't have recognized that. But after months on a ship with scientists, he recognized the difference between the fresh, unused lab and the pitiful mess created by the scientists after they'd settled in.

Here, only basic equipment sat on the counters and larger equipment abutted the walls. Surg walked up to the back wall where a series of large metal doors waited. He walked to the middle one, which had a complex security panel next to it. Kou averted his eyes, allowing the man the privacy to unlock the door. With a thunk and hiss, the door opened, and Kou turned back. The door was thick, a safe most likely. Inside, mostly empty shelves lined the walls. Surg placed the package on a shelf, then pulled the door shut with some effort.

Kou approved. He didn't know the security on the door, but he'd spotted the bolts and thickness. It would take a great deal to get through it physically. Though, he suspected Cass could get through that security panel in a matter of moments…

Walking away, Surg sat down at a desk in the corner and threw his legs up over its surface in a lazy sprawl. "Come, sit." He angled his head toward the nearby chairs.

Kou crossed the room with steady strides, though he couldn't fathom what else the man could want from him. He'd told him everything he knew. He'd given him the rock. What else could there be? His military mind ran in circles, trying to piece together the angles, the motives, but he still hadn't come to a conclusion by the time he sat in the cushioned chair.

Surg laughed. "Relax. This isn't the military. I don't know what you're used to, but we're pretty laid back here."

As he stared at the very successful businessman, he couldn't help but agree. Surg was so relaxed, he looked like his muscles were made of gelatin. Kou leaned back, but his gaze remained cautious. He reminded himself that he didn't know this man.

Though his crew had been contracted by Surg's company, and he'd completed the job successfully, he only had his deceased captain's opinion to go by.

He'd never even heard of Surg or Inia Intergalactic before this job. Having lived and worked near his home world of Ateles, he'd traveled mostly for the military and that rarely sent them to civilized places. This place was definitely civilized.

Surg weaved his fingers over his chest, smiling slyly at Kou. "So, tell me about your lady friend."

Kou scoffed, leaning forward in his seat. "What's with you and my personal life?"

Surg shrugged, the smile remaining on his face. "Living vicariously, I guess."

Kou stared at him, trying to figure him out, but in the end, he just opened his mouth, his life pouring out. "She's a pirate, of all things."

Surg's feet slapped to the ground, and he leaned forward, his smile growing. "What? Seriously?"

Kou laughed. "You could say we had a less than stellar beginning."

"What happened?"

"She stole the package."

"What?" Surg's smile slipped.

Kou nodded. "She hacked the ship's computers and knocked everyone unconscious."

"Even you?"

"Oh, no." He thumped his chest on his organic side. "My lung was seriously burning, but I'm half cybernetic. The other side compensated."

"Interesting." Surg got a far-off look.

"So, of course, I chased after her."

Surg's head turned back in Kou's direction. "Yeah? How did that go?"

He shrugged. "She locked me in the airlock."

Surg howled, slapping the desktop.

"It would have been fine, but we crashed."

Surg jerked to attention once more. "With you in the airlock?"

He nodded. "Complete paralysis, not to mention a really nasty broken leg."

"How?" Surg said, waving his hand at Kou.

Kou tapped his metal cheek. "Nanotechnology. It's installed in all Ateles military personnel at enlistment. It's a lifesaver. Literally."

Surg's slightly elongated mouth hung open, causing his tongue to hang out over his teeth a little. "That is… impressive. I didn't know that."

"Do you know much about the Ateles?"

"I'll admit I haven't given them much thought other than their military might. I always thought they were a little heavy handed."

Kou scoffed. "Heavy handed? Hardly. We do what we must, nothing more."

"And yet your species has developed quite the reputation for its military prowess."

Kou shrugged. "That's just because of our biology and the nanotechnology. Can't be helped. Invariably, beating down a powerful aggressor causes more to come out of hiding to test their own strength. You cannot blame us for that."

Surg nodded. "I can see that. What inspired your people to create such a weapon?"

"What weapon?"

"The nanotechnology."

Kou scoffed again, surprised that such a successful businessman could be so dense. "It's not a weapon. It's a medical device."

"It can't be used as a weapon? It's *never* been used as a weapon?" Surg leaned even farther forward, resting his elbows against the desk.

"Not that I've ever heard. It was created to overcome a weakness in our biology, a debilitating one."

"What was that?"

Kou glared at the man. "I'm not telling you. Military may be given that advantage but few others are prophylactically."

Surg lifted his hands in surrender. "Apologies, though I feel like we got off topic. Didn't this start with you telling me about your lady?"

Kou chuckled, shaking his head. "You're relentless."

Surg shrugged. "How do you think I got where I did in life?" When Kou remained silent, he chivvied him once more. "Well, are you going to speak or am I going to have to guess at where everything went wrong?"

"Where was I?"

"Paralyzed," Surg said with a grin.

"Right. Cass and her sister cared for me as I healed, but we're both stubborn, so things were just as bad after I recovered as before. She kept saying she might try to sell the package to the Diehli." He shook his head. "I still thought she would right up until the moment she double crossed them."

"What did she do?"

"Handed over a counterfeit at the meet then threw a grenade at them." He smirked, remembering the chaos that ensued.

Surg laughed. "That must have delighted your little soldier heart."

"It did. She's… fierce."

Surg nodded. "I suspected as much."

Kou looked up. "How so?"

"How she reacted to her sister's injury. One can't react like that and stay disengaged. It's not possible."

Cass leaned back, letting the cushioned chair suck her in as Jess slept. Now that Jess had woken up, now that she felt confident her sister would live, she felt like all the tension had drained from her body. She was exhausted.

A knock came at the door before Kou's head popped through, his expression hesitant. "Can I come in?"

She sat there staring at him. Should she? Could she possibly make this any worse? Did she want to subject herself to the ass chewing he, by all rights, owed her?

She nodded.

He stepped inside and closed the door, leaning against it. He didn't move forward and didn't speak.

She felt compelled to fill the silence, but what could she say? Was she wrong? Did Jess have it right? She was leaning harder and harder towards yes. Jess had a point. Nothing had been the same since their parents left. Cass couldn't even remember the woman she'd been back then.

She turned back to Kou, watching the hesitant expression on his face, trying to read what was underneath the surface. She knew they were at odds right now. Remembering the scene in medical, she had to admit to herself that she'd screwed up big time. Should she apologize? Again, she was leaning toward a hard yes. She opened her mouth to say sorry, but words failed her, stuck in her throat, unwilling to leave.

"She okay?" He broke the silence, indicating her sister in the bed.

"Yeah," she said. As icebreakers went, it wasn't a bad one. She was tempted to latch onto the subject, push all their problems aside and pretend they didn't exist.

He nodded, his gaze wandering the room.

The silence dragged on. Why wasn't he speaking? Jess said she thought Kou loved her. Cass wasn't even sure she knew what that meant. What the hell was love, anyway? To her mind, it was just another way of hurting yourself.

Maybe that was why she couldn't speak when she tried to apologize. Maybe some part of her was afraid that apologizing would just drag her one step closer to getting hurt. But she wanted to say she was sorry. She regretted her words, but didn't for the life of her know how to say that. How could someone forgive you when you treated them so shoddily?

Or maybe it would be better to explain herself. Maybe if he had a better understanding of her issues, it would be easier to mend this wound she'd inflicted. After all, she had no interest in absolving herself of guilt with empty words. She just wasn't that type of person. She wanted to *fix* this.

Cass looked up, hoping she could get words past her mouth, right before Kou's shoulders sagged, disappointment on his face as he turned and left, leaving her to the silence once more.

"Damn. I did it again."

Why do I keep hurting him?

CHAPTER NINETEEN

Kou lay back on the bed Surg had offered him while he was on the station. He suspected the offer had as much to do with Surg's repeated attempts at matchmaking as anything else. He smiled as he stared up at the ceiling. The man was relentless. He could see why he'd done so well for himself.

Still, it left Kou in this state of uncertainty, nestled in between roles so that he didn't know where he stood. The job was over, his ship and crew gone except for the one woman unconscious in medical.

And he didn't know where he stood with Cass. He felt like that was over too, though he hated to admit it even in his own head.

Why couldn't she have just said something? Anything? She'd just sat there staring at him, like it was already over and he just wasn't getting it. Was it, though? Was it really over and he just wasn't picking up on the signs? He wracked his brain, running through every encounter.

It always came back to that one fight in medical. His mind couldn't let it go, couldn't get past her words. Did she really mean it or was she just lashing out like a hurt animal as Surg had suggested?

Then, an intercom interrupted his thoughts. "Security Specialist Kou, please report to the Control Room immediately."

Kou jerked to his feet, sending bedding flying across the room. He responded automatically to the tone, the wording, storming out of the room at a dead run. He didn't think, didn't pay attention to his surroundings.

Something was terribly wrong. Why did they want him? What could he bring to the table? He wasn't an employee of the station. They shouldn't be calling him to the Control Room at all.

He followed signs leading him onward, his military mind frowning at the tactical disadvantage it gave. Sure, it helped him now, but it also gave enemies directions to their targets. Every military ship he'd ever been on obscured directions, even scrambling obvious paths to slow and confuse enemies.

It took no time at all to run into the Control Room, stopping in front of Surg. "What? What's the problem?" He stiffened his stance as he'd done so many times in the military.

"There're intruders on the station." Surg pointed to one of the screens. "Do you recognize them?"

Kou stepped forward, focusing on the display. He looked at the screen, trying to piece identifying information together, but they gave almost nothing away. Dark gray suits hid most of their identifying features from this angle. The way their faces were positioned away from the cameras did the rest. He shook his head. "I've never seen them before."

Surg nodded, looking grim. "Thanks. I have my suspicions, but I'd hoped you could corroborate."

"Sorry. Do you know what they're after?"

"Not yet." Surg's expression grew darker, a deep scowl marring his face. "They gained access to the station using authorized entry codes."

"A traitor."

Surg stared him down, his gaze deep and deadly. "Exactly."

Kou had no doubt the fate of the one who'd betrayed this man would be unpleasant. The man rose higher in his esteem. Kou looked back at the screen. "What areas branch off that hall they're moving through?"

"It's a main thoroughfare from the docking spoke. They could go anywhere," the tech at the station said.

"Like where?" Kou leaned over the man's shoulder.

"Residential wings, storage and shipping, maintenance corridors, medical."

Kou froze at that last word. No. It couldn't be. "Can you bring up a map tracking the intruders' progress through the station?"

The tech nodded. "Of course."

A second display came alive, labeled with corridor and room designations. As he stood there, the indicator passed maintenance. His gut sank. He looked around him, but no one else seemed to be putting the pieces together.

The timing. It was the only thing that made sense. Jess, Cass, and the traitor's body were all in medical at that moment, vulnerable. "Do you have a comm I can borrow?"

Surg turned to him. "Yeah. Why? Do you have an idea where they might be heading?"

He nodded. "Yeah."

"Where?"

"Medical."

Surg didn't even question it. "Take a team. Tech room is through there."

"Yes, sir." Kou ran from the room, only half noticing the pounding of a dozen boots behind him. He didn't care. He just needed to get to medical.

The tech room was half misnomer. Kou paused for a moment to orient himself. The room was narrow, with gear lockers and shelves lining the walls. At the back, a locked cabinet probably held weapons. Body armor and other non-lethal peripherals lined the left and right walls.

He rushed forward toward the wall holding body armor to the left, his emotions driving him at full speed. His hands shook as he donned each piece. Behind him, he could feel the movement of the men around him. It taunted him with memories, memories of times past, times when he'd still been in the military. The clomping of boots, sound of metal doors opening, clicks of metal against metal, the shink noise of a gun slide being pulled back. It all pulled him closer and closer to losing himself to the past.

Get a grip.

His fists squeezed around the hard material in his hands, material that didn't give as much as he would have liked. It just barely grounded him as he tried to keep his mind in the present. People needed him. *Cass* needed him.

Even if she won't admit it.

He hated that he cared so much, and those emotions he felt for her finally started to pull him back to the present. He looked down at the black material in his hands and continued donning it.

"Sir?" someone said from behind him as a long weapon came into view to his right.

He turned around, taking the gun offered to him. "Thanks. Do we have visuals of medical? What entrances and exits are there?"

The woman handed him a heads-up display. "I assume you know how to use this?"

"New model, but yeah."

She nodded. "Medical has two access points, front and back. If you're right, they're too far ahead. They'll definitely get there before us."

"Is the security system set up to track intruders over the heads-up display."

"Yup. All employees are required to wear trackers. All guests and intruders will show up red on the display."

He nodded, powering up the device. "Okay."

She turned her back, pulling up a display on the opposite wall large enough for all of them to gather round. A map of the facility pulled up, and with a series of touch commands, she narrowed it down to a usable area. He could see the tech room, where one red dot was surrounded by a bunch of blue ones. Next to the room, the Control Room held a lot more blue dots. Random blue dots roamed the halls. Off on the edge of the screen, he saw three stationary red dots—Cass, Jess, and his injured crew-member—in medical and about a half dozen moving through a corridor.

"Okay, if we can move through this hallway," he said pointing at the screen, "we can maybe cut them off."

"Agreed. Okay, let's move out."

<hr>

Alarms blared, jerking Cass from her malaise at Jess's bedside. "What the fuck?" She jumped to her feet, and Jess startled awake.

"What's going on?" Jess yelled over the siren, holding her hands over her ears.

"I don't have a fucking clue." She stomped to the door, yanking it open, but the hallway was empty.

Too empty.

She looked back at Jess and shrugged. "I don't like it. Jess, how you feeling?"

"Okay?" Jess hesitated, sounding unsure.

Cass stepped forward, letting the door fall shut behind her, and touched Jess's leg. "Can you get up? Can you walk?"

"I think so."

"Good, let's get moving. I don't like this." She lifted her arm, speaking into her bracer. "Angus?"

"Aye, Captain."

"Do we know what's going on?"

"Are you asking me to hack the station's computers?" He sounded almost gleeful.

Have I rubbed off on him a bit too much? "Only if you have to."

"There are no warning signals coming from the station and no mobilizations detectable from my position."

"Damn." She fisted her gun, hating being in the dark right now. "Come on, Jess. Let's get moving. I do *not* want to be here if something happens." She would *prefer* being back on her ship. Could they get there? What was going on?

And what about Kou? Where was he? She could barely breathe at the thought of him hurt somewhere, but she shoved the thought aside. He was a security specialist, ex-military. He could handle himself.

"Angus, hack the station. I want to know what's going on, and I want to know yesterday."

"Aye, Captain."

Jess sidled up beside her, hopping to tug on her boots. She didn't bother changing, still in the blue and green dress.

Cass snorted, amused by the picture she portrayed.

"Not funny." Jess glared, crossing her arms over her chest. "Can we go?"

"Yes, of course." Cass lifted her gun to shoulder level and pulled the door open, swinging the gun back and forth to check the hallway. She turned right toward the entrance.

"This place is nice," her sister whispered.

"Not the time, Jess."

"Right," she said, even quieter.

Still, it felt like the sound carried, giving them away. They exited the hall into the waiting room. It was ominously empty, the soothing colors and comfy fabrics somehow eerie with the alarms blaring overhead. It reminded her of scenes in zombie flicks where everyone was dead and yet still walking around, waiting for someone to find this disturbing tableau.

She shivered, wishing her mind would knock it off. This wasn't the time for demented fantasies.

Just get back to the ship.

They would be safe on the ship.

But then the doors burst open, men in dark gray suits pouring in with guns raised. "Get back!" she yelled at her sister as she opened fire. "Get back!"

Kou ran through the halls, heart pounding in his chest, scared to death he would be too late. In his ear, the comm came to life. On the heads-up display, he could see a map of the nearby area, along with the people within that space. They still didn't have a visual on the enemy, only empty gray hallways, but he could see their red dots advancing on the screen.

Too close. They're too close.

They needed to pick up the pace, but they were all running at top speed. He could feel the pull of his muscles, the burn of exertion as he forced himself forward. Like never before, he could tell the difference between his right and left side. One side was screaming at him to slow down while the other just kept chugging forward without issue. For the first time in his life, he wished more of him had been damaged, that more of him was no longer organic. Maybe then he could get there faster. Maybe then he could save them.

"Intruders have invaded medical," Surg's voice said over the comm attached to his HUD.

"Hacht," he cursed under his breath, pushing himself to greater speed, ignoring the signals from his body. Panic set in like nothing he'd ever felt before. He couldn't fail them, he just couldn't. If he lost Cass and Jess, life wouldn't be worth living.

Cass crouched behind an overturned couch in the lobby, shoulder pressed to the slick fabric. Beside her, Jess was curled into a ball, trying to create the smallest profile possible and grimacing as she was forced to hold the uncomfortable position for far too long in her partially healed state. Cass kneeled up, taking potshots at the enemy before dropping down again as more gunfire hammered the furniture.

She'd flipped a table and a couch, using them for cover when they couldn't reach the hall. There was just too much open space. To her left, a puff of cushioning exploded out of the couch, raining down on Jess, who whimpered from her place on the floor.

"Shit."

Jess had wanted to help, to fight, but they only had the one gun. Idiot that she was, Cass had wanted to give the right impression—business-like but prepared—so she'd only brought one gun, spare ammo, and a knife. She knew presentation was important, used it all the time in her dealings with the less reputable, but regretted it now. Damn, she didn't even have her bulletproof jacket on.

When the barrage didn't end, she lifted an arm over the couch and fired randomly, hoping they would stop. They didn't. "Damn it." She leaned around the side of the couch and fired, shooting one guy between the eyes.

As he dropped, she lost her breath.

"Kou."

CHAPTER TWENTY

Kou was terrified as he reached the medical suite, shocked by the siege he stumbled upon. Floor to ceiling windows covered the front of the lobby, giving a perfect view as they approached. They slowed, and Kou gave the signal to stop. The room was a mess. Several of the windows had cracks spiraling out from damage, and one was completely gone, the floor covered in a layer of glass. Gunfire had littered the walls with holes and scorch marks. The room itself was filled with overturned couches, tables, and chairs. Stuffing sprinkled the floor, and there was an almost constant wave of people standing up to fire.

As he stepped in front of the first window, one of the intruders jerked, his head rocking backward and blood spraying out the back of his head. As the body fell, collapsing limply to the floor, he saw her.

Cass's head and one arm peeked out from the side of a couch chewed up by weapons-fire. How were they not dead? Where was Jess? How was he not too late?

Or was he? He didn't see Jess. She could be dead. And for all he knew, Cass could be badly injured and just barely holding on.

From that moment on, he ignored his allies. He rushed through the shattered window, only one thing on his mind—getting to Cass and, hopefully, Jess. If he'd been thinking rationally, using his military training, he would have held back. He would have stayed with the team, methodically making his way through the enemy until not one of them was left standing.

But that part of his mind wasn't in control anymore. All he could think about was getting to Cass, protecting her. The intruders didn't even see them coming, so focused were they on Cass.

Running up on one before him, he raised the long gun in his hands and fired, shoving him aside with a shoulder before he even had a chance to fall. Time slowed, and he marveled when he didn't get shot in the back.

He rounded the corner of the couch. Cass sat with back pressed to the couch while Jess curled in a ball on the floor. "Sweet Atala," he said, body almost going limp. He dropped to his knees and wrapped Cass in his arms, his gun clattering to the floor. He soaked up her warmth, grateful he'd made it in time. Her weapon dug into his chest, hurting, but he didn't care. She was *here*. She was *safe*. Nothing else mattered.

As he knelt there, simply holding her, the battle quieted around them. The panic eased, adrenaline receding, and he finally realized she wasn't resisting him. She was holding him back.

She cursed under her breath as the boss's guest tore off through a broken window, making a beeline for a woman firing from behind the cover of a couch.

He took out one intruder quickly, but that got the attention of the others. "Move it, move it," she yelled, rushing through the shattered window herself.

Her boots crunched on the broken glass as she started firing, quickly sidestepping the opening so others could proceed through. Half the team came one-by-one through the opening while the other half rushed to the double doors a little farther down the hall.

Chaotic shouts joined the sounds of gunfire as the enemy regrouped, trying to find positions that protected them from both the pinned woman and now the dozen security officers swarming in with assault weapons and full tactical gear.

Their opponents wore similar gear to their own, making battle tricky. Even without cover, it would be hard to take them out. But her team wasn't amateurs. They had extensive training fighting people in tactical gear. They knew where most commercial gear was weakest, which spots could be fired on reliably.

Unfortunately, those areas were few and small. Each time she fired, there was a good chance she would miss her target, sometimes only by the breadth of a hair. But they also outnumbered the enemy by more than 2 to 1, and within a diceros, she'd taken out two of them herself with shots to the forehead, breaking straight through the weakest point of the HUD, a seam smaller than the width of her finger.

But anxiety started to build as the couch guarding at least two people continued to disintegrate before her eyes. She edged closer, hoping she could offer additional support to the people huddled behind it.

Before she could get there, though, disaster struck. Everything seemed to slow down while she was powerless to stop what came next. One of the intruders pulled out a new weapon, one she recognized. It was a new model the Diehli had started selling and was rumored to be so powerful it could rip through the walls of a space station.

"No!" she yelled, her gun pivoting to the man. She felt so slow, seeing the gun fire.

A scream cried out from behind her, and she whipped around. The couch's cushioning had exploded in a rain of foam. "Cass," someone yelled in anguish as the boss's guest rose up, right in the line of fire.

Baeki woke up feeling confused. She'd fallen unconscious on their ship as the loss of atmosphere drained her of energy and eventually the darkness closed in on her. When she woke, she didn't know where she was. She didn't recognize the room she was in.

She looked around her, her brain still fuzzy. Light blue walls surrounded her and a light green chair sat to her left, unoccupied. As her brain started to run on more cylinders, she noticed more details. The white sheets. The bright lighting. The sanitation station in the corner with a cabinet above it.

And an unholy racket that sent chills down her spine.

She jerked up in bed, her limbs shaking from the exertion. Her breaths sawed in and out of her, and she battled her instinctual urge to flee.

Where am I?

And why are we under attack?

There was no mistake. Screams and yelling, gunshots, what sounded like small explosions. It sounded like a war was raging right outside her sickroom.

Baeki rose shakily to her feet, using the edge of the bed to steady her. She took several steps, each foot forward a little easier until she could walk unaided by the time she reached the foot of the bed.

She crossed with more speed to the door, opening it just a smidge to check for danger. The hallway, also painted in light blue, was empty, but the sound immediately amplified with the impediment of the door removed. She hesitated, gripping the hard surface tightly as she contemplated her next move.

The hallway was a straight line with no opportunity to hide other than trying to make entrance into the other rooms, which she had no guarantee she could enter. But her room was no sanctuary, either. It was a room with one exit and no opportunity to escape should someone barge in.

Looking down each direction of the hallway, the sound was coming from her right, with subtle movements at the end. To her left, she saw and heard nothing. Her sharp teeth nipped at her lower lip, causing it to bleed. She shook herself, irritated with the bad habit that always seemed to come out when she was stressed.

The left tempted her. It seemed safer, more likely to provide an escape. But her gaze kept drifting to the right, where the noise continued. She tried to convince herself that she was hesitant to turn her back on a potential threat, that it was just self-preservation causing her to keep looking that way. No one who really knew her would actually believe it, though.

You have no sense of self-preservation…

At least, that's what her mother had always said. As a child, her curiosity had always gotten the best of her, and she'd suffered her share of injuries in the process. None of them had ever slowed her down, though. She just couldn't help herself.

"Well, I might as well." She slinked toward the sounds, keeping her side pressed to the wall and hesitating at each doorway, just in case she had to try to dash inside.

The closer she came, the louder it got. She was an aquatic species, so her people were built to listen for sounds muffled by water. She'd always found sounds on land more jarring, but this was downright painful. Grimacing, she continued forward anyway.

Where was she? What was going on? Who was shooting? Who was the aggressor? What did it have to do with the failure of life support or the attack that followed? She could only assume they'd been attacked for the energy source they'd discovered, but she'd never been one to make assumptions, preferring to make an educated guess then immediately test it.

Even if it wasn't pleasant.

She covered her ears as the room at the end of the hall started to come into view. Overturned couches and tables, damaged walls, and loads of debris filled the room she suspected used to be a waiting room. Though hard to see clearly, there were movements behind the cover. The strong scent of ozone filled her nares, telling her that firearms were, in fact, being discharged.

As she reached the end of the hall, she was thankfully still out of sight because of the shape of the room and the focus of the people in it. Combatants with black or gray armor and guns popped in and out of cover, firing off rounds, aiming for somewhere to her right.

Kneeling down, she peeked her head out. From her position, she could see her crewmate, Kou, crouched behind a couch with two other people she'd never seen before. It gave her a momentary sense of relief, knowing she wasn't alone here.

Then something exploded through the cushions. Kou yelled and stood.

Baeki reacted instinctually, screaming out to warn him of the danger.

But her body functioned differently in air than water, exacerbated by her recent illness, and she soon found herself feeling lightheaded from lack of oxygen and blacking out once more.

Kou covered his ears as an ear-shattering noise filled the room. Even covered, he felt like his brain was melting out of his skull. He collapsed to his knees, hunching over until his forehead touched the floor, the cold surface grounding him by the smallest degree under the massive assault.

Then it was suddenly gone, like it never happened. His ears were ringing, echoes of the noise continuing long after it had ended. He lifted shakily to his knees as he checked those around him. "Are you all right?" he yelled, still unable to hear himself.

Cass lay on her back, looking stunned. Blood soaked through a spot on her side. She blinked, then looked over at him. He reached for her injury, but she waved him off, slowly pulling herself to a seated position.

When Cass turned her head toward Jess, he did as well, which was when he spotted his crewmate laying on the ground just beyond where they sat. She was wearing a gown much like Jess was, her long limbs laying akimbo. She was once again pale as she'd been back on the ship.

What had happened?

Had she been responsible for that horrible sound?

More and more people seemed to snap out of the shock caused by that unearthly noise. Kou searched around himself for his gun, which he'd dropped again in favor of covering his ears. Finding it, he lifted it only to find the enemy had reacted faster.

Two of them had lifted the crew-member off the floor, her feet dragging limply in front of them. They used her as a shield as they crept back toward the hallway at their back. They were the only intruders left, but that was enough to take a hostage. He stood, moving his gun to aim at the two, even though he didn't have a clear line of sight. In his peripheral vision, the team he'd arrived with had started moving into position.

The scene seemed strangely calm, like everyone was just waiting, though he didn't know for what.

But these two were not the patient sort. Seeing they were outnumbered, they must not have felt a hostage was sufficient advantage. They started opening fire as they backed quickly into the hallway.

Within moments, an almost constant barrage of gunfire erupted from the narrow hall. The other members of the team ducked behind cover, no longer having the advantage of the intruders' split focus. Agonizing moments ticked by as they each waited behind cover, waiting for a moment to strike.

A moment that never came.

CHAPTER TWENTY-ONE

"Hacht," Kou said under his breath as his crew-member and the intruders moved out of sight.

"My thoughts exactly," Cass said as she pressed into his back, leaning to see into the hallway.

Kou used an arm to move her back as he turned, facing the room once more. All around him was chaos. The team he'd come with were either stationed at the hallway in case the intruders turned back or inspecting the lobby. The armed assailants had left it a disaster area. Nothing had been left untouched. In the aftermath, it was even more macabre, the scuff of boots and clatter of debris somehow obscene in the otherwise silent room.

Ozone hung in the air, filling his nostrils, but surprisingly, he felt okay. He didn't dive headfirst into a flashback. He didn't fall into a spiral of self-recriminations and doubt. For a prolonged moment, there was nothing. He just observed without thinking, without feeling.

The team leader approached, breaking him out of that haze as she spoke. "That hallway opens up on another hallway that leads to the cargo hubs. It's meant for emergency evacuation and receiving supplies."

He nodded. "It has no other outlet?"

She shook her head. "Because medical has the most vulnerable populations on the station, it has a separate evacuation route."

Cass leaned forward. "If that's an evacuation path, I imagine it'll be the fastest route. Also, it's probably a straight shot, so not safe to follow them."

"You're right." She turned around, pointing at the hallway outside the shattered windows. "But *that* will eventually get you to the same place. It'll take longer, but I had all the docks locked down when we identified intruders on board. There's nowhere to go."

Cass smirked. "And I'd bet that route empties into a great, big open space."

She nodded. "It does. Used for unloading cargo or staging evacuations."

"Perfect." Cass stood, brushing off her hands on her pants, unfazed by the wound in her side. "They'll be at a disadvantage."

Kou stood as well, checking his weapon as he did. "Do you know if the area is empty? Is there any cargo they could use for cover?"

"I can check."

The team leader walked away, leaving Kou and Cass alone.

"We'll get her back."

"I know," he said. For the first time in a long time, he wasn't filled with self-doubt. He wasn't questioning himself. He knew that this might not end well, but if it didn't, it wouldn't be for lack of trying.

Kou looked over at Cass, a woman who had happily created a specific framework she operated by that she never deviated from. She went about each job in a methodical manner that reduced risk to both herself and her victims. She never questioned the right or wrong of what she did. And uncertainty never came into the equation, because every detail had been planned out.

Yet when everything went wrong, she didn't hesitate. She acted. She saw what needed doing, asked for help when needed, and kept going. He couldn't say if she'd doubted herself, but she'd never let it stop her. She never froze up like he always did. It made him feel small, until he saw the way she looked at him, both encouraging and concerned. She didn't doubt him, not for a moment.

And neither should I.

Cass stood still, waiting as the lady security officer they'd talked to consulted with command or whatever. Kou seemed deep in thought, but he watched Cass in a way that made her want to help him, even though she didn't know what he needed.

Her ears were still ringing from the noise his fellow crewmember had unleashed. It had felt like a concentrated wave of sound hell-bent on rupturing eardrums. Immediately after, she'd been surprised that her ears weren't bleeding.

The security officer returned. "No, there isn't currently any cargo. It'll be all open."

"Then we need to get moving." Cass checked the charge on her gun. Wasn't great, the charge indicator was an anemic orange color, though not quite red yet. She could still fight.

"What about Jess?" Kou interjected, nodding at her sister on the floor.

Jess immediately pushed herself into a seated position, taking affront at being seen as a burden, most likely. Cass could see how the still fresh wound hampered her, a slight grimace on her face, but she managed to sit up, leaning against the decimated couch. "Don't worry about me. Not like they're coming back, right? I'll just wait here until you return."

"Okay," the security officer said, then pointed at a couple of her men. "You two by the hallway, stay put. Make sure they don't double back. The rest of you, with me. We'll cut them off at the unloading bay."

Cass took up the rear as they filed from the room, boots crunching on broken glass and slipping on pools of blood as they sidestepped the intruders they'd managed to take out.

The march through the monotonous gray hallways left Cass's mind roaming. She stared at Kou's back and smiled, remembering the way he'd charged forward, determined to get to her. She'd wanted to yell, to tell him to stop. Her breath had frozen over in her chest, locked in place by her own fear, as he'd raced to her side among the constant spray of weapons-fire.

It had been stupid and reckless, but she'd never doubted him for a moment. She couldn't say she'd *known* he'd come for her, but she'd also not been afraid he'd abandon her either. She hadn't assumed that he would leave her to her fate. At some point on this journey, she'd come to trust him more than she trusted anyone but her sister. He'd proven himself. Even when he didn't agree with her, even when he was working against her, he was a steady presence that left her certain he wouldn't give up, he wouldn't leave. Whether good or bad, she knew she could count on him.

Cass smiled, then dropped her gaze to Kou's butt, enjoying the show provided by being last in line. After all, she had a reputation to protect, and he did have a fine ass. He also had a tail, which she hadn't paid sufficient attention to until now. Suddenly, she wanted to tease him, maybe flick his tail to see what he would do, but it was hardly the time. Someone's life was in danger, and they were marching off toward an inevitable firefight.

Could you focus for once in your life?

A hand went up in front of her, and suddenly, everyone stopped. Cass took in a deep breath.

This is it.

Her heart started to pound in her chest, making it hard to keep her hands steady. She pulled out her gun from its holster, but it too shook.

Don't be a coward, Cass.

Kou looked back at her, nodding once as if to say, "You can do this."

She took another deep, shaky breath and nodded in return, moving up along Kou's shoulder. "Ready?"

"Yes," he said, almost under his breath. "You?"

"As I'll ever be," she said, shaking her head.

In front of them, the same security officer was directing people into position, the door to the unloading bay closed while they moved. "On my count," she said as another officer waited with hand hovering over the access panel. She counted off with her fingers, then a hand pressed to the panel and the door opened with a hiss.

Without needing to be told, they all aimed through the doorway, focusing their sights on the two remaining intruders who cursed from their position along the far wall, probably trying to board a ship. Cass lowered her weapon. It was too far away for her to hit them with her pistol without hitting the unconscious woman.

"Release your hostage and drop your weapons or we will open fire," the lead security officer said, her voice booming into the open space.

They spun around and yelled back. "Over our dead bodies!"

"That is acceptable." She turned to her team. "Fire at will."

Cass tensed, afraid they would hit the woman in the hospital johnny. It was too far. They were too close together. She flinched as the loud reports of gunfire echoed in the hall, assaulting her ears.

She opened her involuntarily clenched eyelids, seeing one of the intruders down, while the other struggled to get his hostage in front of him, which was when she realized the intruders' mistake. In the hallway before, they'd held the unconscious woman's body between them as they huddled behind her, slowly backing away. But when security had opened the door, they'd still been holding her, but she'd been less cover. One of them had been half holding her off the floor to his side while the other battled with the docking control panel. It had made the one man an easy shot, while the other scrambled to cover himself with the hostage.

Unfortunately, with the woman unconscious and not having a second person there to help lift her, he was too slow and a second crack of gunfire sounded from Kou's gun, causing both to slump to the floor.

Cass let out a sigh of relief. "It's over."

Kou handed his gun off to one of the security officers and wrapped an arm around her. "Yes, it is. Shall we? I'm sure Jess'll like to know how it ended."

Cass hesitated, standing there watching as the team crossed the open space toward the three limp forms. Kou seemed calm, but what about his crew-member? What if she'd been hit? It was such a long distance, and she'd been so close to those using her as a shield.

She waited as someone reached her, checked her vitals, then lifted her up into strong arms. With quick steps, he crossed the space and disappeared into another opening in the wall.

"She's fine," Kou said. "He's probably taking her back to medical. She was still recovering, after all. This'll probably set her back a bit."

"You're right." The officer hadn't asked for a stretcher. Everyone was calm, and he hadn't been rushing. "Let's go check on Jess."

She felt a warmth in her chest as they turned and awkwardly walked back to medical, arm-in arm.

CHAPTER TWENTY-TWO

"I am *not* going back to that bed," Jessie said obstinately, crossing her arms and pouting where she sat on the floor of the mutilated waiting room. Cass and Kou had just returned, and while she worried about the woman they'd rescued, the one who'd been taken hostage, there was certainly no reason to worry about *her.* "I'm fine."

And she was. Mostly. Her shifter heritage meant she could heal pretty quickly. What she *really* needed was a feast. She was *starving* after healing from that bullet wound. The people here in medical hadn't fed her much of anything so far, and she was beyond frustrated. They were afraid she would throw it up.

As if.

"That's fine, Jess," Cass said as she leaned into Kou's arms.

Jessie relaxed and smiled. There was an intimacy about the picture Cass and Kou created in that moment that made her feel they'd overcome their issues. Kou dipped his head to rub his cheek over her sister's hair, and Cass kept touching him in small ways. He didn't even flinch when she touched him on his left side, and even Jessie had noticed he didn't like being touched there.

She hoped they really *had* figured it out. She liked Kou, thought he was good for her sister. Hopefully, he could also keep her in line. Cass was a force of nature, and Kou seemed just down to Earth enough to keep her grounded.

Wanting to give them some time alone, she stood, barely masking her wince as the fresh wound pulled with the movement. "I'm going to head back to the ship to change and get a bite to eat."

"Do you want me to go with you?" Cass said, fear and concern in her eyes.

"No, I'm good." She smiled.

Really good.

"She's entirely too smug," Cass said as she watched Jess leave. She had this nagging feeling she'd played right into her little sister's hands, but she didn't know how or what game they'd been playing.

"Are we okay?" Kou whispered into her ear. The vulnerability in that question broke her heart.

"Yeah." She reached back without looking, running a hand through his hair. Images returned of the fight, of hiding behind a couch that couldn't possibly protect them. "What happened?"

"Intruders." He held her tighter, no doubt having flashbacks of his own.

"Diehli?"

He shook his head, his hair brushing across her cheek. "I don't know, but I'm going to find out," he said, his voice turning to steel. He pulled her to her feet, never letting go. "I'm not leaving this station until we get answers."

Cass nodded, running her free hand over his arm to soothe him. "Sure." It wasn't like she didn't want to know, too. She didn't like the danger she'd found herself in. She might be a pirate, but she'd carefully created a method that bypassed the danger, allowing them to come and go as they pleased. "Let's go."

Kou dragged her out of the room and through the hallways as he talked on his comm, getting the location of someone named "Surg."

He stormed into an ornately decorated office with a man pacing at the opposite end behind a desk. The room was large, especially for a space station. Rich fabrics covered a couch and chairs that circled an intricately carved coffee table. Every surface they passed had at least one trinket that made her fingers itch to grab it and shove it in one of her many pockets.

"What the hell did we step in?" Kou continued into the room, ignoring the bookshelves and art on the walls, and stopping in front of an antique desk.

The man, presumably Surg, stopped and stared at Kou. He had pointed, lupine ears and a slightly elongated face, though he managed to look more businessman than animal. "We're still working that out. I have my people looking into the men you and the team killed." He scowled, his face turning severe. "I have no doubt it is those Diehli." His hands fisted at his sides. "They've been a thorn in my side for far too long."

"Do you think they'll come after us?"

His focus switched to Cass. "I don't know. They went straight for medical, but I don't know what they were after." He shook his head. "They could have been after the body or they could have been after you. Unless we find orders or the traitor, we might never know."

Cass frowned, not liking his answer. She didn't like being on the Diehli's radar. It made her feel exposed, vulnerable. "I can't stay here. I have a life, work."

Surg chuckled. "You're a pirate."

Cass rolled her eyes. "So? It's still work. And I didn't exactly make anything on this venture."

He sobered. "You're right. And you do deserve a reward for turning over the package. I'll get that in motion."

"Thanks," she said distractedly. It felt weird, though. People didn't reward her or pay her like that. She worked for herself, valued her independence, relied on no one.

She looked up at Kou, who still had his fingers entwined with hers.

And yet I have him.

Was she really that independent anymore?

Or was she ever?

Kou was startled that he'd forgotten.

Cass is a pirate.

It had all started with that bit of information. If Cass weren't a pirate, they never would have met. It had driven a wedge between them at first, and yet he'd managed to forget about it entirely.

How could he forget something so important, so vital?

It wasn't like it was something inconsequential. She was a pirate, and that wasn't something he could just ignore. But what could they do? Cass was stubborn, stubborn enough to choose that life over him.

And he feared it might just come to that. She'd stopped resisting what they could have, but that didn't mean she loved him, didn't mean she would be willing to give up her career for him.

And he could never live the life of a pirate. It just wasn't in him. He'd lived his life by the letter of the law, serving his people, serving order. Cass was chaos, but he loved that about her. What did that say about him? What was wrong with him?

He leaned down and kissed Cass on the forehead. "Do you mind if I have a few words in private with Surg?"

She shrugged. "I don't mind."

He watched her as she walked away, not able to pull his eyes from her receding form. When the door closed behind her, he turned to Surg. "I need help."

"With what?"

"What do I do?"

"You're going to have to be more specific."

"Cass is a pirate."

"Yes, you told me as such."

Kou pulled at his short hair, frustrated with Surg. "I don't know what to do. Cass is stubborn, we both are, but I'm not a pirate."

"Ah, I see the problem now." He paused, pacing behind his desk.

Kou watched his movements intently, his mind in turmoil as his conscience warred with his heart.

Surg turned to him, a compassionate expression on his face. "I'll have to think on this."

Kou nodded his head, simultaneously grateful for the help and disappointed he couldn't get an answer immediately. "Thanks."

Kou was different as they made their way back to her ship. He seemed distant even though he'd latched onto her hand the moment he exited Surg's office.

His hand was hot, sweaty even, as they made their way back home. Was he worried about something? What was on his mind?

Finally reaching her bedroom door, she pushed it open, dragging Kou along with her. She stopped in the unusually clean room, not sure where to go. There were the comfy chairs to the left, table and chairs to the right, or her bed straight ahead. Not knowing what was on his mind, she wasn't sure which venue would be best.

She looked back at him, running a thumb over the back of his hand. He was lost in thought, and she turned around again to survey her options. The table would only amplify the distance she felt, and the bed seemed too intimate for the moment, so she crossed the room to the stuffed chairs, encouraging him into one so she could sit on his lap, not wanting any space between them.

Finally settled with her legs dangling off the side and her cheek pressed to his chest, she asked, "What's wrong?"

Silence answered her, and being so hopelessly inexperienced with relationships, she wasn't sure what to do. She couldn't *make* him talk. Even she knew that would only end in disaster. If she were more experienced, she could try to encourage him to voice his concerns, but all she needed to do was think of her relationship with Vicky to know her skills didn't stretch that far.

The silence dragged on, and she accepted it. She let his warmth and closeness relax her. Her muscles released the last residual tension from the firefight, and a small smile crossed her face. *This* was intimacy. *This* was what she'd been missing all these years. It felt like a balm to her soul, and she realized that she wasn't afraid of losing it. She wasn't afraid he'd leave her as her parents had.

"My parents abandoned me," she blurted out. Hearing the words out loud didn't bother her. She didn't feel defensive or dismissive. They were just words. Possibly for the first time in her life, they didn't have power over her.

"Oh?" Kou said, his body tensing slightly under her.

"I was just barely an adult, and Jess was just a little kid." She sighed. "One day they just weren't there anymore. I was angry for a long time. I tried to keep it from Jess, tried to provide for her, protect her, but I couldn't. I didn't trust anyone but my sister, and I didn't open myself up to anyone but her either."

She laughed. "Well, that's not quite true. I latched onto Vicky and Ellie like a lifeline. When Vicky got emancipated at sixteen, I took her under my roof, even though there wasn't any room for her. I clung to them like my life depended on it. Suddenly, I'm wondering if I did them a disservice."

With gentle fingers, he lifted her face up. "Do you think they wish you weren't in their lives?"

She shook her head. "No, but I suspect I'm a pain from time to time. I'm certain I drive Vicky nuts. She's not exactly the most social person. But I start freaking out when I haven't heard from her in a while. Intellectually, I know she's probably just deep in her work or being antisocial, but a part of me panics."

"You worry she's leaving you behind."

"Maybe."

"And maybe she needs you. Maybe she needs you to keep her connected. She lives on that ship alone, with no contact with other beings. I believe people need to know others are thinking about them. They need to know they have value."

He paused, and Cass pulled back, watching him closely. He seemed deep in thought, like he was wrangling with his own inner demons.

"Tell me," she said.

He focused on her again, though he seemed hesitant.

"It's okay. Just tell me." She shrugged.

"You know," he tapped his left side, "how I feel about this."

She nodded.

"Ever since the battle that took the rest of my unit and half my body, I've felt like a failure."

Cass opened her mouth, wanting to object, but held herself back. She suspected he needed to speak right now, not be reassured of his worth. Settling back into his lap, she rested her head against his shoulder, thinking a lack of eye contact might help. "Go on," she whispered.

"I blamed myself for their deaths. I couldn't accept the way people looked at me, like I was brave, a hero. On my world, these metal scars are considered a testament of strength, of someone who's gone through something terrible and come out the other side stronger. And having half my body replaced? I was looked on with a level of awe I just couldn't accept.

"I left the military, but even then, I couldn't handle it. My scars reminded me every day of the ones that didn't survive. Yet to everyone else? It was something to be praised."

"That's why you were on that ship?"

"Yes. I needed to get away. At least on a multi-species crew, not everyone saw it the way most Ateles do. It didn't solve the problem, though. I constantly second-guessed myself, causing me to constantly check and recheck my work. I was methodical, precise, and was praised for it, but again, I didn't feel it was deserved. I always felt like I was one mistake away from completely falling apart.

"I don't know why, but being with you has helped. I've seen how you've handled everything, things you weren't equipped to handle, but you did so with grace."

Cass snorted at the idea of being called graceful. "Sorry."

"You've accepted me, had faith in me."

She sat up again. "Maybe it wasn't me. Maybe you were just ready."

"No, it was you. If we hadn't met, I'm pretty sure I would have still been on that path. I think I needed you to shock me out of my own head."

She smirked. "Well, yeah, I could definitely see myself shocking someone." The smirk shifted into a gentle smile. "You know, before you, I had no interest in repeat performances."

"I know."

She raised an eyebrow. "You did?"

He nodded. "Your sister told me."

"That little witch!" She moved to get up, but Kou held her in place.

"She wanted to protect me from getting hurt."

Cass sighed. "She wasn't wrong." She looked away. "I think I felt like I couldn't get hurt if I didn't let people in. I was quite the horndog."

"I have no idea what that means."

She leaned in. "How about sex fiend?"

"That translates."

"Thought so." She leaned back and chuckled. "It drove my sister nuts. I have a tendency of playing racy audiobooks in public spaces on the ship, much to her chagrin.

"You're the first guy I've made myself vulnerable to since my parents left."

Kou pulled her into a hug, his big arms unyielding, and she curled even closer to him.

"I don't know what did it, and I'm probably still fucked up, but I don't want you to go. I don't want to lose you. I've gotten stuck on you, and I want to see it through."

"You're not fucked up," he said as his arms momentarily flexed tighter. "A little broken maybe, but we both are."

She looked up at him. "Maybe that's why this works."

"Maybe, but does it matter?"

"Not one damn bit."

"Captain?" Angus whispered, dragging Cass awake. Kou was holding her tight from behind, his entire body curled around her in his sleep.

"What is it?" she whispered back, trying not to wake her partner.

"An Inia Surg is requesting entry to the *Trojan*."

Cass frowned. Was that the man they'd met earlier that day? What would he be doing here in the middle of the night?

Or maybe it *wasn't* the middle of the night. Damn, space travel was such a pain. She looked over her shoulder at Kou and lifted his arm as she slid out of bed. She held her breath as she scooted forward, but as she got to her feet, Kou merely curled against her pillow, oblivious. "Phew."

Cass grabbed the first clothes to touch her hands and walked into the hallway. "What's his demeanor, Angus?"

"Relaxed, though I can only gather so much information from an unidentified species."

"You mean to say you've been here for days and you haven't managed to learn everything there is to know about this station and solar system?"

"He's not from this solar system."

"Right," she said as she walked toward the airlock, wondering where he *was* from. "Okay, I'm in the cargo bay. You can let him in."

"Aye, Captain."

She finished her trek to the airlock as the inner door opened, revealing the man from the office earlier. "Welcome to the *Trojan*," she said, reaching out a hand.

He looked down at her hand in confusion, and she dropped it to her side.

"It's a greeting on Earth."

"Ah, I see."

Cass leaned against the wall behind her. "So, what brings you to my ship?"

His gaze sized her up and when he spoke, she figured she'd passed muster. "I have a proposition for you."

She smirked. "Well, that's a loaded statement."

He seemed confused again, but continued anyway. "As you may have guessed, my company has a strongly antagonistic relationship with the Diehli. And I don't anticipate that changing any time soon." He scowled, hands fisting at his sides, and started pacing. "Recent events have made it quite clear that we're not equipped for the depths of depravity our competitor is willing to go to."

She snorted. "Meaning they'll use any dirty-handed tactic to get what they want and you won't?"

He stopped and stared her down. "How someone goes about something is just as important as the end result."

Cass felt like she'd been slapped. Did he think she was no better than the Diehli? Sure, she was a pirate, but even she had standards, things she wouldn't do.

"It pains me to say this, but something needs to change. We can't keep going the way we have. Nearly an entire crew we contracted was killed." He shook his head. "I've always tried to do the right thing. I've worked with governments when I could have made more money commercially, all because it served the greater good." He shook his head again. "I can't let this go unanswered."

She pushed off the wall. "What do you plan to do?"

He stared at her, trying to read her. "How would you like a job?"

Cass frowned. A job? Why the hell would she want a job? "What?"

"Kou has told me something about you. From what I've heard, you have standards, limits, that fit well within my own morals, yet you aren't afraid to get your hands dirty when needed. You get jobs done that others would pull off by more treacherous means. I need someone like that. I need someone I can turn to, someone I can count on, when the Diehli cross the line."

"What do you want from me?"

He smirked at her. "Use your powers for good instead of evil?"

Cass chuckled, but for some reason didn't dismiss the idea outright. "I'll think about it."

Surg nodded and left.

Cass continued to stare at the door long after it closed. She loved her independence and chaffed at the idea of working for someone, being under their heel.

With a sigh, she turned to walk back to her room, continuing to dwell on Surg's offer.

There was one big problem. Working for someone else just didn't sound like her. Sure, it would have been nice to fuck up the bastards who crashed her ship. She chuckled, shaking her head. She did kind of fuck them up already. A big grin stretched her face at the thought. Guns, bombs, and grenades, oh my!

As she slowed her steps, not ready to return to her room just yet, she could admit to herself that those bastards she'd taken out were a symptom, a branch of a much larger tree. Taking out a single ship and a few henchmen wouldn't do squat against a big corporation.

But that wasn't her problem. They'd *made* it her problem for a spell when they came after her, but that time was over. Unless they attacked again, she had no reason to go after them. Cass could go about business as usual, leave the Diehli be, and wreck havoc on the universe somewhere far from here. She wasn't the righteous sort, after all, she told herself as she pushed her way into her room. She froze, staring at Kou's sleeping form. Even with his cybernetic parts, he looked so soft and carefree in his sleep. Somehow, she couldn't keep thinking those thoughts with him in front of her, and she felt paralyzed.

Because he is *righteous.*

The thought came to her out of nowhere. "Oh damn," she whispered. He was too good, too honorable. How could he possibly be happy watching her steal from others to make ends meet? It would slowly rip them apart.

She remembered how they were at first. They were at each other's throats, with Kou demanding she return the package, and Cass stubbornly refusing. That would be them every damn time she started a new job.

It wasn't a future she wanted.

But could she change for him? Did she even want to?

She sat down on the side of the bed, running an idle hand through his hair. "Kou," she said, leaning down to kiss his temple.

He groaned, his arm reaching out to pull her closer.

She laughed, smacking him playfully. "Not now, Kou."

He opened his eyes, his left a stark blue that stole the show with his face half buried in the bedding. "Morning," he mumbled.

"Hey, hot stuff."

"What are you doing out of bed?"

"Got a visit from Surg."

He looked adorably confused. "What did he want?"

"He offered us a job."

"A job?"

"Yeah." She leaned forward as she continued speaking. "He said he needs someone with our skills to help him with the Diehli."

"Our skills, huh?" he said, smirking.

"Well," she replied, "mostly me."

He smacked her ass. "God, I love your sass."

"And I love your ass," she said, grabbing a big fistful.

He laughed, the sound booming through the room. "You love more than my ass, woman."

"I do. I really do." She kissed his lips, then his cheek, lingering on the metal there, a reminder that it didn't matter, that she accepted him. "Are we good together, Kou?"

He grabbed her chin and turned her to face him. "We are perfect together. Who else would put up with us?"

She laughed, holding him tight. "Asshole!"

"Pirate."

"Damn straight!"

EPILOGUE

essie stretched as she leaned back in her chair in the cockpit, using the big screen to review the latest documents from Inia.

This is fun.

It was some sort of corporate espionage. They needed to retrieve some stolen information and wipe all records from Diehli computers. Her sister could probably pull that off in her sleep.

She smiled. Things had been interesting since leaving the space station. Cass and Kou had finally figured things out, though Jessie couldn't say it was any less hectic around here. With Cass, things were never calm, and Kou was just as stubborn, so an explosive argument happened every day or so.

Unfortunately for Jessie, those fights were always followed by epic make out sessions and obnoxiously loud sex (mostly) behind closed doors. Jessie sighed and rolled her eyes. That was the only downside to having Kou around. She and her sister used to be partners in crime. Now, Jessie felt like a third wheel, a third wheel suffering miserably from a bad case of TMI.

"A call is coming in from Victoria," Angus said, interrupting her musings.

"Oh, nice. Put her through," Jessie said, leaning forward in her seat. She always looked forward to talks with Victoria, even if the other woman was a bit spacey.

The screen came alive with Victoria's face looking off to the side, her black hair pulled back in its usual ponytail.

"Hi, Victoria!" she called out, waving at the screen.

Victoria jerked her head to the camera. "Oh, good. The call went through."

Jessie grinned. "Did you think it wouldn't?"

Victoria shrugged, but couldn't hide a grin. "I wasn't really paying attention."

"What's got you so excited? No, wait." She turned around and yelled. "Cass! Kou! Victoria's on the line!"

On the screen, Victoria smiled, unable to sit still. It wasn't like her, and it made Jessie curious. What had her in such a good mood?

Cass stomped into the room. Jessie looked behind her, laughing at how her sister was still straightening her clothes. It was either laugh or cry. She'd gotten over her squeamishness about her sister's liaisons pretty quickly once Kou moved in permanently. She just couldn't avoid it anymore.

"Fly's undone," she said, pointing at Kou's crotch.

He flinched, looking down and discretely fastening his pants.

Jessie smirked and turned around. "Okay, we're all here. What's got you so excited, Victoria?"

"I had a breakthrough." She shook her head, her hands waving in the air. "It's big. Really big. This could very well change the way we look at space travel."

"Really?" What could it be?

She nodded. "Uh huh. I've been working on this for so long, I can't believe I'm there. I still have to do some testing, but I think it's just a formality."

"You're not really going to leave us hanging there, are you, Vicky?" Cass said, her weight pressing down on the back of Jessie's chair. "That's just mean."

Victoria laughed. "No, I'll tell you." She shook her head. "God, this is just..."

In the background, Angus's voice came through on Victoria's end of the call. "The communications channel has been compromised."

Victoria flinched, eyes widening. "I have to go. Sorry." She reached forward and cut the connection.

"What the hell was that?" Cass said, smacking Jessie's headrest.

Jessie looked behind her.

Kou crossed his arms, looking stern and every bit the military man. "Trouble."

READY FOR MORE?

This series will continue with Victoria in Shifting Paradigms.

Victoria just wants to be left in peace. But when an malicious corporation shows an unhealthy interest in her latest invention, what she needs most is the last thing she'd ever want…

Now Available for Pre-Order

GET 2 FREE EBOOKS

I love building relationships with my readers. As part of that, I regularly send emails with deleted scenes, never before seen excerpts, pre-order and new release announcements, and more.

If you sign up to receive these emails, I'll send you <u>Mila's Flight</u>, the prequel to the Darkest Day series, and <u>Shifting Sides</u>, the prequel to the A Shift in Space series, FREE.

Join Now to Get Your Free Ebooks

www.theeternalscribe.com

DID YOU ENJOY THE BOOK?

If so, you can make a **BIG** difference...

Reviews are among the most important tools in my arsenal for getting my books in front of readers like yourself. I'm just one person. No matter how much I shout, my voice can only carry so far.

But do you want to know what does carry?

A crowd.

When one voice joins another who joins another, that matters. *That* gets heard.

Let your own voice be heard by leaving an honest review. It only takes a few minutes, but makes a major difference not just to me as an author, but to readers like yourself who are trying to decide on their next read.

Thanks again!

Danielle

ACKNOWLEDGMENTS

A special thanks to my dad for providing feedback for editing and Avery for suggesting the name Chad Sexington.

ABOUT THE AUTHOR

Danielle Forrest is a Paranormal SciFi author and Medical Laboratory Scientist based out of Indianapolis, IN.

She has dedicated her life so far to two things:

Science & Books

So it really shouldn't be a surprise if science finds its way into even the most fantastical examples of her writing.

Sign up for her mailing list at www.theeternalscribe.com to get access to exclusive content and updates.

facebook.com/theeternalscribe

twitter.com/theternalscribe

instagram.com/theeternalscribe

goodreads.com/theeternalscribe

amazon.com/author/danielleforrest

bookbub.com/profile/danielle-forrest

ALSO BY DANIELLE FORREST

THE DARKEST DAY SERIES

Mila's Flight

Mila's Shift

Tristan's Choice

Terra's Fate

The Darkest Day Collection

A SHIFT IN SPACE SERIES

Shifting Sides

Shifting Cargo

Shifting Loot

Shifting Paradigms